MIND OUT OF TIME

by

CHRISTOPHER STASHEFF

ISBN-13: 978-1-953215-10-9
ISBN-10: 1-953215-10-6

Published by Stasheff Literary Enterprises, Edgewood, NM, USA
Visit us at http://christopher.stasheff.com.

Table of Contents

Introduction

I've been making up stories as long as I can remember, but I never took that vital step of writing one down until I was a senior in high school. I look back on that first story now and the way it has grown into its own novel (never finished, never submitted) and see themes that have emerged in my science fiction—the head versus the heart, the individual against the institution, the necessary illusion in conflict with the destructive delusion—and wonder how much my writing has really changed.

Well, I started writing science fantasy, of course. At first I thought I couldn't, because writing SF meant you had to know something about science—but in the 1960s, when the New Wave broadened science fiction to include topics outside the scope of physics, chemistry, and biology, my own knack for combining science and fantasy became not only permissible but also appropriate to the times as the boundary between fantasy and reality has began to blur in the Computer Age. Today, people form friendships with others whom they've never seen, in personas that may not even exist. In fact, one physicist told me, fifteen years ago, that in his research, it was beginning to look as though whether a particle was matter or energy might be a matter of viewpoint.

As my work has progressed, though, I have found emerging a conviction that no matter how the settings of our lives may change, the way people deal with one another will not. Sure, behavior will take new forms, but there will always be misfits, always those who put themselves before anyone else, always those who are willing to sacrifice themselves for others, and in spite of all this, most people will have as their main motivation the wish to find a group to which they can belong and someone with whom to share their lives. However, I have come to believe, as I have grown older, that for some, those goals are wrong. They find other goals, the goals that are right for them, that are equally fulfilling.

Mind Out of Time reflects that search, those themes, and that conclusion. Doc Angus is delighted to have any kind of social role at all—but isn't sure if he wants it to infringe on his individuality. There is also, in his story, a sense of destiny, of the old Anglo-Saxon concept of the "weird," the unseen trap that waits for each of us—a social role we are born to fulfill, a life's work we exist to achieve. Those who find it and embrace it succeed in life, though sometimes in terms the rest of us can't understand; those who never find or refuse their weirds will never really be happy or content.

I hope I have found my own weird in interacting with my fellow human beings and in writing stories from the inspirations that result. I hope

further that Angus McAran's tale will be some help to those of you who
are still searching—or resisting.

— Christopher Stasheff, 2011

Neanderthal

PART I

The whole thing probably wouldn't have happened if Angus MacAran had been born like other kids. But he was a breech birth, came out feet first. It set a precedent—the rest of his life, he went at everything bass-ackwards. His whole personality was built around perversity; maybe that's why he could understand people so well.

Also, he was born of Halloween. That might have had something to do with it.

Even then, nothing probably would've happened if his body had been standard. But it wasn't. Right arm a few inches too long, left leg a few inches too short—he looked as if his whole right side had been shifted up about three inches higher than the left. His shoulder was about on a level with his ear and there was a large lump of muscle on it; he called himself a hunchback. And his right leg was three inches shorter than his left, so his shoe-sole was a trifle thick. Add to that a head two sizes too large for his body, and he could make the rest of the world seem out of balance.

He grew up scrawny. His hair was always thin, and so blond it seemed white, with eyebrows of the same ilk, over hard, sharp bone. His eyes were so pale they scarcely seemed to have any color at all, and they were set way back under hard, sharp brows in a perpetual glower. His nose would have looked more appropriate on an eagle, and his mouth never smiled.

He was deformed. He knew it, and would allow no dodging of the point; he was deformed, and said so. He was not an "exceptional person" or an "extra-normal" or a "special;" he was deformed—and if anyone called him anything else, he shut them up fast. "Cripple" he would allow, or "grotesque,"—but never "handicapped."

Especially not "handicapped." Physically, he had to admit they had a point; he wasn't exactly built for sports and, in the Midwest, that meant he wasn't exactly built for socializing.

So he grew up a loner. By the time he got to high school, the other kids were willing to be friendly—but he could tell they were trying, so he wasn't. Three years later, when he hit college, solitary living had gotten to be a habit, and he'd developed an intense interest in machines—they were so easy to understand, compared to people. So he majored in electronics and computer science and, having a unique, off-center viewpoint, he managed to come up with a few concepts the professors had overlooked. He had patents (pending) on several very interesting devices before he even graduated, Class of '44.

Yah. A genius.

At least, when it came to dealing with electrons. With people, all he had was a lively interest. But that was very lively; being on the outside, he had a huge hunger to find out what was going on inside. So he took large doses of anthropology, psychology, and sociology and, to catch what the scientists missed, he added literature and history. So he had a good grounding in theory, but when it came to the practice of getting along with people, he was still inept—unless there was a good argument going on that he could work his way into. Then it was his idea that counted, not his personality.

Defense mechanism? Of course. He'd been carrying the shield around since he was five and, by the time he realized it'd expanded into a complete suit of armor, he'd lost his monkey wrench. He had to wait for someone to come along with a can opener.

So he stepped out of college lonely and compensated for it by diving into his work like a mole. He was an electrical engineer, and a brilliant one; he was also a physicist. There aren't too many men with that combination, and when there are, they're usually spelled "inventor."

Which he was. He was also 4-H, a major consideration back in the Sixties—so InterContinental Business Mechanisms swallowed him up the instant he took off his cap and gown, put him to work in Research & Development twenty hours a week at a fat salary with full benefits, and paid for him to go to graduate school with the rest of his week. By the time he hit thirty he had a whole barrel of patents filed for his company (which paid him quite well for the privilege). No royalties of his own yet, but ICBM paid him $100,000 a year to "do research" for them—not bad, in the Sixties—and marketed at least two new products of his design every year. They made quite a profit on McAran.

So they didn't mind at all if he was unruly—he could, if he wanted to, come in at two A.M.; that was fine, and the guard wouldn't ask any questions. If he didn't want to show up at all, that was fine, too. He wanted a fully-equipped laboratory in his home for the days he didn't feel like coming in? Fine, nothing easier. Terminal installed in his study with a dedicated line to the mainframe at the lab? Sure, but shouldn't he let them add a bigger study to his house so he wouldn't feel cramped? A secretary? No problem. Did he want her at home, too? No? Well, how many lab assistants? What flavor, male or female? None at all? Was he sure? Well—how about a cyclotron?

But he didn't have women. He wouldn't have anything to do with them; he was deformed, and he knew any woman who gave him a smile had eyes on his wallet—any woman he found attractive, anyway. Oh, there were a few who showed genuine interest in him—but he did have certain minimal standards of appearance and intelligence, and he was sure that any women meeting those standards was bound to be interested him only one aspect of his character, and it was green and gave a crisp crackle when you folded it.

So he didn't like company. His youth in the schools on the wrong side of town—there hadn't seemed to be any right side, for him, and he'd tried enough schools to know—had convinced him of that. It'd been worst in high school and college, where the other students showed pity and concern, however well-masked (and it hadn't been until high school). At least in grade school his classmates had been honest. He'd had the bruises to prove it—and still had the worst ones, there on his ego.

Which was why he lived like a pauper. The only thing he really wanted was ownership of the patents on the machines he invented—which he didn't have. What else would he spend money on? Girls? He wanted them, sure—but all he knew how to do with them was argue. Steak? Vintage wines? He thought of food as fuel. Luxury? He didn't have time for it.

No, the only thing he wanted was to be his own master (and collect his own royalties). That took money—but not just enough for a comfortable living; that much, he already had, just from interest. No, he meant to keep on doing R&D—but for himself, not for ICBM. With the kind of projects he worked on, that took money, big money. So he was hoarding every penny against the day that he could open his own company. That's why he lived in a three-room apartment in an old building, stayed home nights winding weird coils and sketching arcane designs, took all his vacation trips at the library, and socked every penny into blue-chip stocks and gilt-edge securities. The only thing he spent money on was clothes, and that was only because it was company policy.

Lunchtime a week after his thirtieth birthday, Angus was twisting his way through the crowded commissary at I.C.B.M., looking for an empty table and an argument, the kind where ideas counted for more than personalities. Even at thirty he was still very much aware of his three-inch sole and twisted shoulder and couldn't believe anyone could really enjoy talking with him. So good arguments were his only form of socializing.

"Yeah, I saw that skull," said a deep voice off to his left. "Sure it looks like a Neanderthal—but they dug it up in Michigan!"

That was all Angus needed. He veered to his left, zeroed in on the table with the three men and snapped, "I saw it, too! And with that kind of prognathism and the occipital lump, you're gonna try and tell me it's anything but a Neanderthal?"

The speaker looked up, surprised. He was broad and beefy with a shock of black hair, heavy brows, and almost no chin. "No, matter of fact," he said slowly. "I wasn't trying to tell you anything at all."

"Uh, Yor," said Tal Drummond nervously, "this is Angus McAran, Cybernetic Electronics. Angus, Yorick Thall." Then, before either of them could get a word in: " 'Scuse me. Gotta get back to the lab." He left, hurrying a little.

So did the other two men at the table. They'd been through Angus's arguments before.

Yorick raised an eyebrow. "Just you and me, huh? All right, I'll bite."

"I doubt it." Angus sat down. "Yorick?"

"An ancient and honorable moniker." Yorick nodded. "You didn't think Shakespeare invented it, did you? …Say, aren't you the young hot-shot with all the patents?"

"Older than you, I'd guess," Angus snorted, "and InterContinental's the one with the patents; I just invented the gadgets."

Yorick nodded. "Accounting appreciates it."

"So does InterContinental," Angus said sourly. "Now, about…"

"Yeah, so much that they gave you your own lab, plus full tuition and all the time you wanted to work on your doctorate." Yorick grinned. "You can't hide much from the boys with the books."

"Except book-learning. You don't know much about anthropology."

Yorick shrugged. "I've got a running interest in Neanderthals."

"Then stop running and start reading. How could you say that new skull at the museum isn't Neanderthal?"

"Because they've never found a Neanderthal in the Western Hemisphere." Yorick turned serious. "And this is a new skull; they just dug it up last summer. Sure it could be Neanderthal—but it's no older than some pre-Indian remains they've found. So it could just be an Iroquois ancestor with a funny-shaped head. Or it could be a hoax."

"And if it's not, the anthropologists'll have to throw out one of their main theories." Angus smiled, too sweetly. "Right now, every prof in the country claims Neanderthals died off before they could reach the Bering Straits bridge—and they hate like hell to have to admit they were wrong."

"No, not really," Yorick said thoughtfully. "What they do hate is to say something's true before they've got all the facts."

"This skull's a fact. And they didn't have it."

"What fact?" Yorick shrugged. "There're men walking down the street today who look like Neanderthals—and some of them are on their way to the executive suite. Could be we're all descended from hybrid Neanderthals with Cro-Magnon spouses. Not surprising we occasionally look like our ancestors."

Angus sat back, regarding Yorick narrowly. "You do have a point…"

"Yeah, and I'm a great example of it. I know." Yorick's mouth tightened; then he shrugged. "So I've got a personal interest. Doesn't stop me from being right."

"But it doesn't give you an occipital lump." Angus smiled tightly. "Only genuine Neanderthals had 'em—and so does this skull."

"And modern humans don't." Yorick pursed his lips. "There, it gets sticky…"

"And you can't pull it out." Angus slapped the table and sat back triumphantly.

"Not without doing some research. But if I sampled a hundred thousand modern skulls, I bet I'd come up with a few occipital lumps."

Angus waved a generous hand. "Do it, by all means. Study modern Neanderthals. Sounds like a good way to get to know more about yourself."

Yorick's face set into grim lines. Then he smiled sweetly. "Beats studying gargoyles."

Angus paled, his eyes growing huge in his head.

Then he threw himself to his feet and turned away.

"Oh, stick around," Yorick said softly. "Convince me I'm wrong."

Angus turned back. "Don't worry, I will."

"How? By proving the skull's a Neanderthal?"

"Yes!"

"How?" Yorick grinned. "Gonna hop in a time machine and run back a few hundred years to interview him?"

"Yes!" Angus whirled away and stalked out of the commissary.

Aacthuu stood watching the last of his clan stride over the ridge into the setting sun. At his feet lay a slender, flint-tipped wand, snapped and broken.

"A tool of demons!" choked the grizzled old spear-maker, staring in horror at heresy.

"Get away!" snarled his mother, nursing the baby. "Out from our sight, twisted brat! The sight of you so frightens the child, she will not suck!"

"You are no spawn of mine," growled his father. "No, you shall not hunt! The noise of that twisted foot would warn the game."

Aachtuu was strong as a man, though he was only twelve; his shoulders were huge with far more muscle than a natural child should have. And he was quick, but that was his undoing—for when the twig along the forest path snapped back into his face, and the mocking laughter of the other boys rang about him, he could only think that here was power, to be had for the asking.

"It is a plaything of the demons," spat the old spear-maker.

The patriarch looked down at the flattened spear-shaft, bowed by a thong. He lifted one of the slender miniature spears and snapped it in half. "Our men are virtuous hunters," he rasped. "They have no need of the toys of Darkness."

"He is no spawn of mine," rumbled Aachtuu's father.

"Out with him," snarled his mother.

"Out with him!" shouted the clan.

"I cast him out," growled the patriarch. "Let him seek abode with the great-toothed cats!"

Angus was pretty sure he could travel in time—but he'd never dared try it. After all, he might not come back. Which wouldn't be all that bad, except...

His body would stay in the Twentieth Century. Without a mind.

But some considerations outweigh fear—for instance, anger.

He stomped into his dingy three-room apartment, locked the door, turned on a table lamp, hung up his coat, loosened his tie, took off his shoes, and sat down on the floor in front of the coffee table. He closed his eyes, forcing himself to breathe slowly and deeply. When the blood had stopped pounding in his ears and a measure of calmness had returned, he opened his eyes and stared at the conversation piece on the coffee table.

A Klein bottle.

Consider a Klein bottle. On second thought, don't; there are safer sports.

You've seen the beast—a three-dimensional Möbius strip or, if you prefer, a three-dimensional model of a four-dimensional object. It's a bottle whose neck loops around and plasters its mouth against its side. But it doesn't stop there—it goes on to the bottom and opens out in a flare like a trombone bell. And the hell of it is that, if you put your finger on the surface and follow its curves, you find your finger coming out from the bell, up over the side and around the neck, and down into...

Right. Into the inside.

So where's the outside? Yes—inside. And the inside is outside. And...

You see the danger. If you really get contemplative and study a Klein bottle long enough, sooner or later you find yourself beginning to wonder if maybe your outside isn't really on your inside, and vice-versa, and...

...and the room seemed to be darkening around the Klein bottle, slowly, gradually, until only it remained. Then it darkened, too, and disappeared, leaving only darkness. Angus hung floating in a sea of night, surrounded by blackness shot through with concentric patterns of electric color, swelling and disappearing while new ones formed

Angus took a deep breath and let calmness roll over the beginnings of fear. He'd learned meditation from an excellent teacher, but he knew he hadn't studied anywhere nearly long enough to be trying anything more. This far he'd been before, many times, and felt the familiar cold lump in the center of his being, the lump of fear and near-panic, pulsing there under a very thin blanket of tranquility. Maybe winning an argument wasn't so terribly important after all...

Then he realized that he could see all around him—without turning his head. Before, behind, above, below... he could see everywhere; his peripheral vision encompassed a sphere.

Fascinating!

He forgot his panic.

Now—how?

How could he have wraparound vision without wraparound eyes? His fear submerged under the delight of a problem.

He frowned pensively, lifting a hand to rub his chin...

Nothing happened.

Irritated, he sent the neural command to his hand again.

Again, nothing happened.

Angus clenched his jaw in annoyance. To be bothered with details, at a time like this...

Then it hit him, and the cold of space shot through him. Not down his spine, just through him, like an arctic breeze through a fog—for he had no body.

Fascinating!

Angus tensed every muscle in his body, one by one.

Nothing happened.

He grinned. So that was why he couldn't lift a hand!

Then he frowned, remembering something he'd heard about astral body travel. He didn't think that was what this was, but just in case, he imagined a string, imagined very hard—and it glimmered into being, from his heel all the way down to wherever his body was, where it joined with his body's heel. Just in case.

Well, theory validated. So what else was new?

Stars.

The patterns around him faded, stabilized, and he found himself looking down on a string of lights, like a highway at night, a long line of glowing dots, strung out like streetlamps and, away off to the side of his vision, a dim glow, as though there were other lights over there, if he'd just turn and look...

But one problem at a time. Angus frowned figuratively, chewed his mental lip thoughtfully. Let's see... he'd intended to travel in time, and he'd hoped the Klein bottle meditation would shoot him into another dimension, from which he could look down on Time as though it were a road map.

Excellent. His subconscious had come through for him, providing him with that same analogy for a perceptual framework. Well done, Subconscious; he couldn't possibly have comprehended this Limbo as it really was.

So. He was in another dimension. If (*IF*) Time was the Fourth Dimension, then he was in the Fifth... But the exact number didn't matter. He was in another dimension. Period.

So why hadn't his body come along?

Because it was three-dimensional.

Then obviously, his mind wasn't. Very interesting.

But scarcely vital. Back to the analogy.

He looked down on the line of lights again. They, obviously, represented Time, and each light marked a given period—say, a year.

He frowned, a sudden thought occurring to him. Slowly, he shifted his "visual" focus off to the side, toward that dim glow. There was another line of lights over there, angling toward his own. He followed it with his "vision," saw it converge and join with his own time-line a little way "back..."

He'd heard about alternate universes, of course. That other line, then, would be the time-line of an alternate universe, and the point where it merged with his own universe's time-line would be the date of some huge cataclysmic event which had caused one time-line to split into two. Perhaps, in that alternate universe, the Third Reich ruled the world...

Angus shuddered.

Or maybe Adolph Hitler had died of influenza right after World War I.

Suddenly an intense curiosity gripped Angus, the old craving for knowledge. Maybe a quick visit...

But not right now. His thoughts veered back to the project at hand—going back in time about twenty thousand years.

Okay, this was his native time-line. Which way was the past?

Well, if time-lines split at major events and diverge, the two time-lines growing farther and farther apart as time goes by, then the point where they join is the past. Beyond the first junction he could see another time-line and, dimly beyond that, a third. Angus lifted his viewpoint and saw the time-lines spreading out like the branches of a tree—and where they came together they seemed like arrowheads pointing the way toward the past.

He thought briefly of the future, decided regretfully that it would have to wait for tomorrow, and got down to the problem of travel.

How do you move without a body?

The people who dabbled in astral-body projection didn't seem to have much trouble—but they, at least, had bodies, albeit astral. This state Angus was in was clearly a totally different avian species. Experimentally, Angus thought of motion, imagined the lights below him moving, streaming past. After all, it was his analogy, wasn't it? So he ought to be able to manipulate it any way he wanted.

But how far could he stretch that analogy?

Well, he was going to find out soon. The lights below had begun to move.

Slowly at first, then faster and faster, the time-lights below rushed past him, accelerating at an ever-increasing rate, becoming a blur—faster still, faster and faster, till the blur had become a single, solid bar of light. Universe junctions flicked past him as Angus shot back towards the Paleolithic.

Angus had no way of figuring the date—but he did notice that universe-junctions became fewer and farther apart as he went back in time. With a little rapid figuring, he decided that the younger history became, the fewer cataclysms people would cause, which meant it would be the disruptions of Nature that would cause more and more universe-divergences.

In other words, universes diverged only rarely until humanity began to become civilized.

So as soon as the distance between junction points had became greater, Angus let himself sail on three-fourths of the way to the next major junction (which, he figured, just might be the human migration across the Bering Straits) and stopped.

Now what?

He frowned, chewing his imaginary lip. If he could manipulate his analogy any way he wanted...

He imagined the stream of light-points flowing slowly under him until the exact date he wanted was directly below him.

Again, the lights began to move—which meant, of course, that *he* was moving. He counted a hundred fifty-seven light-points going by, then...

The string of lights stopped.

Angus smiled, feeling a little smug. He hadn't been too far off, after all.

He frowned at a sudden notion—this was all a little too easy. The chances of his choosing the right point on the first try were not exactly large. Could there be some other intelligence around, helping him, guiding him—for its own purposes?

Angrily, he thrust the thought away, tried to forget the feeling of Antarctic cold that gripped him. *How to get down?* he thought firmly. *How to get down?*

Well, it had worked so far, so...

He imagined the point of light growing larger, moving up at him—and sure enough, it did!

Again, he had the eerie sensation of some other mind guiding him as the light grew closer, but thrust away the feeling with a snarl, then forgot it as the light-point seemed to reach out, pulling him into itself. Angus felt its tendrils touching him; there was a momentary sensation of falling, of being engulfed, pulled into—

A Klein bottle.

Before him sat a Klein bottle.

Angus blinked, stupefied.

Then his prefrontal lobes reasserted themselves. A Klein bottle? In the far past? Impossible!

Obviously, then, he'd gone in the wrong direction; he had to be in the future.

"No, you're in the middle of the last Ice Age."

Angus jumped, felt his body lurch, and…

Body?

He looked down, feeling a head tilt on a neck—and saw a body.

A body. Not his.

Who it did belong to would be rather difficult to say—but, judging from the hair, the guy must be second cousin to a grizzly bear.

"It ain't much, but it's all I've got."

Angus jumped again, then glared around him. Whose voice…?

"Mine," it answered. "Who're you?"

"Angus McAran," Angus snapped. "Who…"

"Doc!" The voice was jubilant. "Damn, it's good to hear you again! Been a hell of a long time! How you been doing?"

"Oh, not bad, not bad at all," Angus muttered, a little dazed. "Work is getting a little heavy, haven't had any inspiration in a long time, but aside from… Hey! Hold on a minute!"

"Okay. Sure." The voice sounded puzzled, maybe a little hurt.

"All right." Angus took a deep breath. "Now. Who are you? And where am I?"

He looked around again as he said it. He seemed to be sitting in a cave in front of the Klein bottle. A small fire crackled in the cave-mouth; beyond it was a starry sky over silver moonlight on a snowfield.

But he didn't feel cold; there was a thick fur blanket over his shoulders. He fingered the robe, wondering how much of the fur was robe and how much was his body. "Also—what am I? And what the hell is that Klein bottle doing here?"

The voice was cautious. "Uh… you don't remember, Doc?"

"No, I don't remember!" Angus snapped. "And stop calling me 'Doc!' "

"Oh." The voice was quiet a moment. Then, "You're not a Ph. D. yet?"

"No! Absolutely not! And even if I were, you don't think I'd admit it, do you?"

"Matter of fact, yes," the voice said cheerfully. "You're too honest not to."

"How the hell would you know?"

The voice was silent again; then, "Uh, Doc—is this your first time-trip?"

"What do you mean, my first..." Angus made a choking sound, eyes bulging. "You mean..." He cleared his throat. "Oh... I'm going to do a little more time travel?"

"You might say that, yes. Actually, you're going to organize GRIPE."

"I've organized a lot of gripes already, and I don't mind letting people know about 'em. Is there going to be something new about this one?"

"Uh, could you go a little lighter on the sarcasm, Doc?"

"Don't call me *Doc'!*"

"All right, all right, I'm sorry! Forgive my existence!" The voice took a long, patient breath. "Yeah, there is going to be something new about this GRIPE you're going to come up with, Do... uh, Angus. Uh, all right if I call you 'Angus'?"

"Of course," Angus said impatiently. "Get on with it, will you? What's this new gripe of mine?"

"Oh, yeah, that." The voice paused a moment. "Well, you see, GRIPE stands for 'Guardians of the Rights of Individuals, Patentholders Especially.' "

Angus winced. "Who dreamed up that title?"

"You did," the voice said promptly. "Or will, I should say—my past, your future. You know how it is."

"Uh, yes." Angus didn't. "And, uh—just what kind of organization is this?"

"Oh, it's a network of time-travelers."

The cave was awfully silent for a minute.

"Angus?" The voice sounded anxious. "Still there?"

"Uh, sort of." Angus shook himself to disguise a shiver. "It seems I'm getting caught in my own network, doesn't it?"

"Mmmm... interesting way of putting it," the voice said noncommittally. "Might be more valid, psychologically, than either of us would like to admit..."

"Keep your validations out of my psychology," Angus snapped. "I suppose this means you're one of the time-travelers?"

"Of course," said the voice. Then, contritely, "Sorry, Doc—I should have introduced myself earlier. I'm Alasper."

"Alasper?" Angus frowned. "That sounds familiar."

"It should; you named me... or *will* name me, I should say."

"Maybe I won't," Angus growled. "Or do you think you can tell me what to do?"

"Noooooo—just predicting…"

"Comes to the same thing, doesn't it?"

"Not at all, really," Alasper assured him. "You're going to decide to do it of your own free will."

"How can it be my own free will if I've already been told I'm going to do it?"

"How should I know?" Alasper sounded smug. "I'm just a time-agent, not a philosopher. Besides, your future self only told me the what, not the how or the why."

"Sure you're not a philosopher?" But Angus's curiosity was up. "Uh, what's this future self of mine going to be like?"

"Uh…" Alasper considered the question. Then: "Well, I can tell you this much, anyway: you're going to develop a sense of humor."

"Me!!?!??"

"Believe it or not. Why else do you think you named me 'Alasper'? Or gave me this last assignment, for that matter. And it's a real boffola, too—going on right now. Practical joke, of course—but it's the best you've ever come up with."

"This, I could believe," Angus growled, "but I fail to appreciate the humor. Or is that just because we haven't gotten to the punch line yet?"

"Uh, no, it's because you didn't hear the straight line. See, I'm a Neanderthal."

Angus stared, astounded.

Then a nasty suspicion began to creep up on him. He cleared his throat. "Uh—yes. A… Neanderthal."

"The real thing," Alasper said modestly.

"Um," Angus hedged. Then, "And this is, uh… Michigan?"

"The Irish Hills, to be exact," Alasper confirmed. " 'Course, the frost is a little thick right now."

"Yes, of course. And may I ask what you, a Neanderthal, are doing in Southern Michigan?"

"Well, that's where it gets funny."

"So far I'm not laughing. What's the joke?"

"The joke is me."

"I might be inclined to agree, if I knew you a little better." Angus scowled. "So far, though, I am not amused."

"Well, you bet me—excuse, you're *going* to bet me—that a Neanderthal couldn't make it from Prague to Detroit in less than twenty years."

"I take it you won."

"Hands down; I made it in ten. Then in 1959, some professor is going to dig up my skull, and you're going to laugh yourself silly watching the anthropologists go into conniptions. Funny, no?"

"Hilarious," Angus muttered. "So I doom you to a life of perpetual isolation just for a joke? I don't think I'm going to like me."

"True," Alasper admitted. "But then, you never did. Don't worry on my account, though. Actually, you see, this is pretty late in the Pleistocene, and the Bering Straits migration is almost over. I come from a holdout pocket of Neanderthals up in the Alps—almost as much of a curiosity in Europe as I am in America."

"And the Folsom-point people have worked their way down to Michigan by now?"

"Yep. Their descendents will be the Huron Indians eventually, I suppose. That's going to be your doctoral dissertation, by the way."

"Dissertation?" Angus looked up hungrily. "Doctorate?"

"Yep. Something to do with electronic testing of prehistoric human remains—magnetic resonance or something. *The Origin of the Wyandotte Nation*, by Angus McAran, Ph.D."

"Ph.D.," Angus echoed dreamily.

Then he snapped out of it. "Ridiculous! I'm an engineer, not an anthropologist!"

"Yeah, but this is the electronic proof of genetic links."

"Stuff and nonsense! Besides, what evidence would I have? I'm not about to go digging up twenty-thousand-year-old graves!"

"No, you'll have ancient battle sites to excavate—anything that we'll bury for you to find for you to leak to anthropologists thirty thousand years from now."

"Oh." Angus thought it over a moment. "Uh—a little unethical, isn't it?"

"To analyze bodies that were abandoned on the battlefield? Probably not unethical, as long as you give them a decent burial when you're done— or have the current members of their nation do it, if you can be sure which people they're from."

"No, no! ...Well, that too, of course. But I was thinking of you telling me where to find them."

"Possibly," Alasper hedged, "but I don't think the academic community would believe you if you told them the truth."

"That's not exactly new." Angus's lips pressed thin. "But even overlooking that, it doesn't change the fact that you wind up holding the bucket, 'a stranger and afraid...' "

"Uh, before you get too maudlin," Alasper interrupted, "would it help any if I told you I'm not afraid?"

"Not much," Angus growled. "I still leave you isolated."

Alasper chuckled.

Angus bristled. "What's that for?"

"I'm not exactly alone," Alasper explained, amused.

Then Angus felt his arm reach out to throw some twigs on the fire and panic surged in him. Someone else was controlling his body!

But the twigs caught just then, and the fire flared, glowing warm on a golden face. Angus looked up…

And caught his breath, eyes widening.

Alasper chuckled again, softly.

She was round-faced and Asian-featured—not Eskimo, not Indian, but something of both, with a large measure of Mongol thrown in. Her eyes were large, her lips full and generous, her skin golden. Black hair framed her face, billowing down to her lap in lush, full waves.

"Pretty?" Alasper murmured.

"Beautiful," Angus breathed.

"Her tribe didn't think so." There was grim anger in Alasper's voice. "By their standards, she's scrawny, and too skinny-hipped to possibly bear a child. None of their men wanted her—so she came to the ugly, bestial stranger who fell in love with her. Me."

Angus swallowed, with difficulty.

"So don't fret your conscience, D… Angus. You had—will have—my interests at heart."

"Reassuring," Angus mumbled, but envy and longing and loneliness ached in him. "Uh… can I talk to her? What's her name?"

"Nacha. But no, don't say anything, Angus. She's still meditating."

"Meditating? Oh! The Klein bottle. You concentrate on it, and…"

"…it opens us to the next dimension, yes."

Angus nodded, chewing his metaphorical lip. "Do you do this often?"

"About once a week, in case any GRIPE agents want to get through."

"So," Angus mused, "each point of light I saw is somebody in a trance?"

He heard a snap and looked down to see his hands breaking a stick of kindling and throwing it into the fire. His scalp prickled. "Uh, Alasper… I didn't break that stick. I mean, I didn't, but my hands did."

"*My* hands," Alasper corrected.

"Oh, yeah…"

"Yes, naturally. After all, this is my body, Angus. But you're welcome to share it for a while."

"Thanks." Angus felt numb. "Then the human body can't travel through time?"

"Not without a machine," Alasper confirmed. "But the persona can. See, you can measure a body in three dimensions—but did you ever try to measure your ego?"

"No, but they're working on it," Angus said absently. "So while I'm in your time, I share your body?"

"Right. And all this time we've been talking, we haven't really been *talking*."

"Telepathy?"

"Yeah, the easy way—share the same brain."

"Share the… uh…" The full implications hit Angus. He swallowed hard and hoped his adrenaline reaction wasn't bothering Alasper's body. "Uh… Alasper—I hate to bring this up, but… Neanderthals couldn't have had a concept like 'ego.' "

"False assumption," Alasper said easily, "not that it matters. See, I had a modern education—*your* modern. Matter of fact, you taught me."

"Traveled back in time and taught you," Angus mused. "And you just taught me about time travel, and… Look, don't you think this is getting a little redundant?"

"Definitely," Alasper agreed, "and it's a pretty big mouthful to try and swallow at one sitting… um… Speaking of mouthfuls—Nacha should be coming out or her trance pretty soon, and she roasts a boar haunch even better than I grill a caribou steak. Care for a bite?"

"Uh…" Angus frowned. "How can I…"

"Well, I'll eat it, but we'll both taste it."

"Uh, maybe some other time." Angus let the sight of Nacha register thoroughly in his memory and hoped Alasper couldn't feel his surge of envy. "I think I'd better be getting home, Alasper. This has all been a little overwhelming."

"Don't let it get you down, Angus—it's only this tough the first couple of times. After that, you get to recognizing the landmarks—Caesar crossing the Rubicon, the Crucifixion, Constantine seeing the Sign, Charlemagne, William of Normandy—all the major forks in the road. Get to be like old friends after a while."

"Definitely a great consolation," Angus said sourly. "Uh… I really will finish that dissertation, huh?"

" 'It is written'," Alasper quoted. "So long, Angus. Drop in any time."

Then he was gone. Angus spoke sternly to the chills down his nonexistent spine, took a deep, metaphorical breath, and plunged into the future, counting on his figurative fingers.

If Angus had bothered going into work that next week, his co-workers and his supervisor would have been very worried. He was even more withdrawn than usual. What was worse, he was scarcely hostile at all—just depressed.

He sat in his apartment gazing out the window but seeing only the time-line, and when restless energy built up, he went out and wandered the city in a black brood, forgetting to eat for days at a time. He logged lots of hours in coffee shops in front of untasted cups, glowering into their murky depths.

Fortunately, he didn't have any friends to be worried by his strange behavior—and his few acquaintances tended to steer away when Angus got moody.

Which was just as well. The young man was holding so many imaginary dialogues in his head that there wasn't much room for real ones.

So it came to pass that, as Angus sat brooding over another untouched, cooling cup, a chair scraped and a heavy body jarred the table as it sat down.

Angus's head snapped up, life coming with anger. Couldn't they leave him alone?

He clamped a hold on his forebrain.

Yorick sat, grinning, across from him.

Angus focused his brood into a glower.

Yorick sipped from a steaming cup, set it down. "That ceremonial skull really bugging you, huh?"

Black rage roared up in Angus. "No, I'm not worried about that damn skull! And where the hell do you think you get off, sitting down here without being invited?"

"Yeah, I know," Yorick sympathized. "Really bugs me when strangers move in unasked, too. But I'm not a stranger, remember? I'm Yorick."

"I don't give a damn who…" Angus broke off, staring at the broad face. Sloping forehead, heavy brows, receding chin… A fine-mesh grid suddenly formed behind Angus's eyes, comparing each minute detail of the face before him with the contours of the skull in the museum. His Pleistocene host had called himself Alasper…

Yorick…

Angus winced and thought about leaving a nasty note for his future self.

Yorick was frowning, concerned. "*Now* what's with you?"

The question sounded honest—and of course, Yorick was a lot younger than "Alasper" had been…

Time travel could do strange things. Somehow, Angus couldn't doubt that Alasper and Yorick were one and the same.

So the meeting with "Alasper" was in Angus's past and "Yorick's" future. Younger, but the same man.

And, therefore, a GRIPE agent.

And he had hunted Angus out.

Angus bristled. He was not going to be conned into founding a time-travel organization in which he had absolutely no stake!

His eyes narrowed. How to make the big lug admit it...?

Yorick eyed him sidewise, as though he were trying to remember the number of the local mental hospital.

"Where were you born?" Angus rapped.

"Prague," Yorick said, surprised.

Then he saw Angus's slow smile and understood. For a moment, there was a guarded look in his eyes.

Only for a moment, though. Then he was saying, "Course, my folks emigrated when I..."

Then he shut up, because Angus was laughing too loudly to hear him.

For a moment, Yorick reddened; then his face settled into a careful, rueful smile.

Angus cut off the laughter. "You were raised in this country, of course."

"Of course." The smile stayed.

"How long did it take you to cross the Bering Straits?"

Yorick frowned, confused; then his eyebrows shot up. "I'm going to cross the Bering Straits?"

Angus's face congealed. "You... didn't know about that?"

Yorick shrugged. "They don't tell us anything more about our personal futures than they absolutely have to. So I'm going to make the long hike, huh?" His lower lip thrust out; he nodded, resigned, bleak.

"Tough luck," Angus said with satisfaction. "Must be cold."

Yorick shivered. "You don't know *how* cold, Doc... I mean, Angus!"

Angus ignored the slip, except for a slight grinding of the teeth.

"Sorry," Yorick said quickly. "It'll take me a little while to get used to calling you 'Angus.' "

Angus's eyes narrowed a little. "Didn't take you long to drop the pose, did it?"

Yorick shrugged. "I didn't figure it was the best policy, anyway. Only too glad to come honest, when it turns out I had to."

"But you didn't have any choice about the pose, huh?"

Again, the shrug. "Orders."

"From whom?" Angus rapped.

"You, of course." Yorick seemed surprised. "Or, well, your older self. Doc."

Angus stared, shaken for a moment.

Then he remembered the business at hand and managed a glare. "And you're supposed to con me into setting up this time-travel organization?"

Yorick squirmed. "I wouldn't exactly call it a con..."

"Oh? What would you call it? Ethical persuasion?"

"Not even that." Yorick met his eyes with a frank, open gaze. "I'm just supposed to make sure you consider both sides of the question. Any time you come up with a reason why you shouldn't set up GRIPE, I'm supposed to give you a reason why you should."

Angus smiled sweetly. "In other words, talk me into it."

"Well…"

"A con."

"No," Yorick said judiciously, "just making sure you hear our side." He smiled. "Nothing unethical about that, is there?"

Angus was still trying to think up a reply when Yorick suddenly stiffened.

Angus frowned. "What…?"

Angrily, Yorick waved him to silence. His pupils expanded: then he said softly, almost whispering, "Do you hear something ticking?"

"Ticking?" Angus said blankly. Then he glanced at his watch.

"Not there." Yorick stood, shoving his chair back. He knelt, wrapping huge hands around the single central column that supported the table and lifted it slowly. It was a hollow pipe and on the floor beneath it, there was a small, black sphere with a tiny clock-face set into its surface.

Angus still couldn't hear the ticking.

Yorick nodded with satisfaction. "About what I figured."

He picked up the little black ball, put down the table, and strolled out of the coffee shop, whistling.

Angus stared after him. Then he surged to his feet and followed in a limping run.

He caught up just as Yorick stepped through the outside door, swung his arm in an excellent overhand pitch, and sent the black spheroid high into the air. Angus watched as it came down in the middle of the little park next to the coffee shop. He frowned, perplexed.

Yorick hummed cheerfully.

Angus turned on him. "Was all of that really…"

His voice trailed off as he saw that Yorick was looking at his watch and counting seconds on his fingers.

Angus felt the cold lump of fear seeping into his belly, so his voice was doubly harsh. "What the hell is all this a—"

The blast slammed him against Yorick's broad chest and rocked the concrete under his feet.

The little park lay in ruins, a haze of smoke rising over a huge new raw crater.

Angus clawed his way back up from his hands and knees, staring at the torn earth in numbed horror.

Then he realized Yorick's hand was on his elbow, had helped him to his feet. Slowly he turned, his eyes round as egg yolks, staring open-mouthed at the Neanderthal.

Yorick nodded, his face grim. "You've got a few enemies, Angus." Abruptly, he smiled. "That's the real reason I'm here, y' see—to make sure you stay alive long enough to found GRIPE."

That brought Angus out of his daze, at least partly. "If I decide to."

" 'Course." Yorick slung an arm around his shoulders, half holding him up, and turned to burrow through the crowd to the door and back inside. "Think you could use a cup of coffee?"

Angus stumbled with him, trying to make his brain function. "But... but who? Who'd want to kill me? I mean, it's got to be someone I know, at least!"

"Not yet," Yorick assured him. "But you will. You will."

Angus gazed numbly at the flashing red and blue lights through the coffee shop windows. Just police—no ambulances, thankfully. It was midmorning, apparently the perfect time for a bomb to go off; all the kids were at schools, their parents at work, and the park empty. Yorick handled the routine questioning masterfully, with just the right blend of innocence, shock, and bewilderment. The officers soon moved on, leaving Yorick free to casually lead Angus away to a different coffee shop.

While Angus's tremors were subsiding over a new cup of coffee, Yorick explained the *real* situation in a low voice. "Y' see, Ang, it's like, uh... You don't mind it I call you 'Ang,' do you?"

"Ang? uh... buh... wuh... uh, Sure! Uh, yuh."

Which was about the only way Yorick could've ever gotten Angus to agree to the nickname.

"Well, y' see, Ang, it's like this—there're three time-travel organizations going."

"What!!?!"

Yorick nodded. "The Society for the Prevention of Integration of Telepathic Entities—they're anarchists, pretty much; the Vigilant Exterminators of Telepathic Organisms—they're totalitarians; and, of course, GRIPE—uh, that's yours."

"Uh. Mine. Yuh." Angus was still a little groggy.

"And, of course, it's..."

"Wait a minute!" Angus snapped out of it. "That last one's mine—*if* I decide to organize it!"

"Of course," Yorick said equably. "But at the moment, you haven't definitely decided *not* to found it, so it does exist." He hurried on while Angus was trying to unsnarl the double negative. "And, naturally, SPITE and VETO are fighting it."

"Oh, yeah?" Angus bristled. "Where do they get off fighting my organization? We weren't hurting anybody, just sitting there minding our own business, no bother at all, and these guys got to… *Wait* a minute! I haven't even founded the damn thing yet!"

"Well, let's not sweat the details," Yorick said easily. "Now, GRIPE has been doing a lot of good up and down the time-line—but SPITE and VETO are the bad guys, see, so they don't like good, and…"

"All right, so they don't like GRIPE," Angus growled. "Will you can the kindergarten stuff and start being a little more objective?"

"All right, all right!" Yorick sighed and leaned back. "You geniuses are so particular… Well, let's put it this way: GRIPE has done a lot to further democracy."

"Why?" Angus snapped.

Yorick looked up, surprised. "Because democracy does a better job of protecting the rights of individuals, especially patentholders, of course. And they're the ones GRIPE's most interested in."

"Oh."

"And since democracy protects them better than any other form of government, GRIPE does all it can to further democracy."

Angus lifted a skeptical eyebrow; he suspected someone was being less than completely honest, and it wasn't Yorick. "I suppose that makes a certain sort of half-baked sense…"

"Yeah, well, you have to remember our founder when it comes to things like that."

Angus glared, but Yorick plowed ahead, grinning. "Anyway, that's why the bad guys don't like us."

Angus frowned, not understanding.

Yorick sighed and took out a cigar. "Remember I told you SPITE was anarchistic? Well, it goes beyond that—they're actually pretty much the time-travel arm of a permanent anarchistic organization. Mostly ci-devant aristocrats in their membership, and…"

"What!?!!"

"Of course." Yorick blinked in surprise. "In practice, anarchy always turns into warlordism—and the nobles like that, 'cause it makes each one of 'em a petty king."

"Oh." Angus thrust out his lower lip. "*That* kind of anarchy."

" 'In practice,' I said. Of course, their manifestos are very pure doctrine, but they all know how much that's worth." He lit the cigar, puffed thoughtfully. "Well, they've got a few purists in there—real idealistic, poor suckers."

" 'Suckers'?" Angus cocked his head to the side.

Yorick shrugged. "The aristocrats know pure anarchy can't endure more than a few months, so they know the idealists are no threat. But they also know idealistic fanatics can be very useful, and make very good agents."

"Yeah, I've noticed puritans are usually pretty fanatical," Angus mused, nodding. "What about the other organization?"

"VETO." Yorick exhaled a cloud of smoke. "They're the time-travel wing of a permanent totalitarian organization. Also doing everything they can to kill democracy. Of course."

Angus nodded, frowning. "And GRIPE is the time-travel branch of the permanent democratic organization?"

Yorick shook his head in the middle of his own private fog. "Only by coincidence. GRIPE's an independent organization. It's just that it's got common interests with democracy, so it helps out where it can."

Angus rocked his head back on one shoulder, looking askance at the Neanderthal. "No formal connection at all?"

"Not even an informal one." Yorick smiled. "You might say GRIPE is private enterprise."

Angus frowned. "Seems there oughta be something in the way of agreements."

Yorick chewed on his cigar, choosing his words. "Well, Ang… Hate to tell you this, but there ain't no really permanent organization of democrats, nohow."

Angus stared, unbelieving.

Yorick shrugged. "Figure it out for yourself. Actual, viable democracies are few and far between, and they don't last as long as empires or feudalisms. They can't, since they're the product of social-force stresses. And, where you've got a stress…"

"You've got a rupture," Angus finished. "Sooner or later."

Yorick nodded, looking pretty bleak.

"But there's gotta be some kind of permanent organization!" Angus exploded. "For self-defense, at least!"

Yorick shrugged. "All these permanent organizations are pretty far in the future, Ang. SPITE was formed in 5237 A.D."

"*Was* formed?"

"Was," Yorick said firmly. "You'll get used to it."

"I'm not sure I want to."

"Don't worry, you will." Yorick went on hastily, "Of course, I can't say for certain the democrats haven't organized on a permanent basis, some time in the way far future—but if they have, they haven't let us know about it."

"So," Angus said slowly, "to all intents and purposes, GRIPE is the permanent democratic organization."

"Closest thing to it, anyway," Yorick agreed.

Angus scowled at him; it seemed to him that the Neanderthal was watching him very closely…

A chill ran down his spine. He was beginning to get an idea of just how much of a load they were trying to shove onto his shoulders. "No!" His fist slammed down on the table.

Yorick was all surprised innocence. "Why?"

"Well…" Angus looked away, fumbling for words, feeling like a heel. "It's too much responsibility, damn it! I'm not going to have a load like that on my back!"

"Sorry, Ang." Yorick grinned. "You've already got it. If you decide 'no,' you'll have to live with yourself afterward."

Angus glared, furious.

"Besides…" Yorick waved his cigar expansively. "You're already paying the price. Why not get the goods?"

Angus's eyebrows tangled in consternation. "I'm not paying any price!"

"You have already."

Angus stared.

Yorick nodded slowly. "Unpleasant things happened to you, all your life. Now you know why."

Angus glared, the storm clouds gathering.

"Now you know the reason, Ang." Yorick smiled sympathetically.

"What… do… you… mean!"

"Why do you think you've got that extra leather on your shoe?"

"That has nothing to do with time travel." Angus's lips barely moved. "There's no possible connection."

Yorick only smiled.

"And I am not going to found your damn organization!" Angus's fist slammed down on the table.

"Right," Yorick said agreeably. "You're going to found *your* organization."

"No! I'm going to live my life the way I want to—nice, average, plain, dull life with no bigger responsibilities than anybody else ever gets!"

"If you survive," Yorick nodded with enthusiasm.

Angus's face emptied.

After a moment, he said, "Survive? Survive what?"

"Bombs," Yorick said casually. "Rifles. Knives. Poison, falling objects, lasers, speeding cars. Human beings ain't so durable, Ang."

"But… why?" Angus managed to croak. "Why, if I decide not to found GRIPE?"

Yorick shrugged. "As long as you're alive, there's a chance you'll change your mind and found it after all. That's why SPITE and VETO are doing everything they can to bump you off." He puffed on his cigar reflectively. "Two huge organizations, bending all their resources to killing your own sweet self, Ang... it's one hell of a compliment. If you look at it right."

Angus shivered.

"Time agents, all up and down your time line," Yorick mused. "All your life..."

He puffed on the cigar, giving his words time to sink in, watching out of the corner of his eye as a look of stark terror seeped into Angus's face. Then he asked, "Any close brushes with death?"

"Huh?" Angus's head snapped up. "Hell, yes! All my life! I damn near didn't get born, even! Breech birth, and all of a sudden all the equipment in the operating room went on the fritz, and..." His voice trailed off, horror drowning the terror in his face.

Yorick nodded somberly.

Angus wrenched his gaze away, clasped hands twisting.

"Averages out to two major attempts on your life every year, Ang," the Neanderthal said quietly. "So far."

"But... but..." Angus floundered. "How could I have survived this long?"

Yorick's laugh was dry, mirthless.

Angus looked up at him, surprised.

"You don't think GRIPE's about to let you get killed before you've had a chance to found us, do you?" Yorick's smile regained some warmth. "Oh no, no way. We've been watching out for you all along, every minute of your life. Not that we haven't had a few failures—but we've managed to keep you alive."

"And maneuvering me into doing what you want!"

Yorick stared. "Of course not, Ang! Just kept you living, that's all. You'll do the rest all on your own!"

Angus smiled sourly. "And if I don't?"

Yorick pursed his lips. "Well... I don't suppose we'll ever know about it. Myself, I'll have died when I was twelve years old."

"Emotional blackmail," Angus said through his teeth.

"Nothing fatal, though." Yorick chewed his cigar. "At least, for you. Anything like an 'accident' isn't too hard to handle. But a man with lead underwear and a piece of plutonium in his pocket—that's another matter. Enough of them got through to cause the fetus some pretty heavy damage..."

Angus stiffened.

"…hunchback, shortened leg, unequal…"

"All right, all right!" Angus snapped. He glared down at his clenched fist. "Bastards…" He looked up suddenly, wide-eyed. "Hey! That radiation… what did it do to my mother?"

"Well…" Yorick's mouth twisted. "Didn't improve her health any…"

Angus's eyes burned. "She died when I was in high school, and my father didn't seem too interested in living, without her… So I owe them his death, too…"

Yorick's jaw clenched.

Angus frowned, puzzled; then his eyes widened. "Oh, no, hold on! It makes a great story, but all you had to do was find out my biography and you could fabricate it to order!"

Yorick looked up, surprised, then weary. "Why would I make it up, Ang?"

"To get me to do what you want!" Angus snapped.

Yorick rested his forehead in his palm, shaking his head.

"Prove it," Angus challenged, "all of it."

Yorick looked up, his face bleak. "I hadn't realized you were always this pigheaded."

Angus glared. "What do you mean, 'always'?"

"I mean, your older self is," Yorick explained, "but I figured that was just because he's getting old and crotchety. Seems I was wrong."

Angus smile was thin. "Not completely. He's getting old and crotchety. I'm still young and crotchety. And stubborn."

Yorick closed his fist, nodding, his face sardonic. "From Missouri?"

"Jug-head mule," Angus agreed. "Show me."

"All right." Yorick straightened, laying his hands palm-down on the table-edge. "Check the facts. It all hangs together."

"Except for this." Angus raised a finger. "From what you've said, I shouldn't have managed to survive at all."

Yorick stared, appalled. "Ang! I told you GRIPE wasn't about to let you get killed, didn't I?" He tried to smile. "No, no, not a chance! Look over there—the little man with the violin."

Angus followed Yorick's nod and saw the musician in the corner.

" 'Aura Lee'," Yorick said, "just the way you like it."

"Thanks, but I think I'll sit this one out." Then Angus looked again. "You mean… he's keeping an eye on me?"

"Just a precaution."

"He's one of yours, then?"

"Oh, yes," Yorick said. "Him, at least, I recognize."

"You mean you don't…" Angus frowned. "No, of course you wouldn't recognize all the enemy agents."

"A few," Yorick said. "One or three. Until they realize we're onto them and get plastic surgery."

"Seems kind of drastic."

"It's pretty standard, in the fifty-eighth century," Yorick said.

"But not in the fifty-eighth B.C.!" Angus stared as realization struck. "You're here!"

Yorick stared back. Then he looked down at himself, body, arms, kneecaps… "Yeah." He looked up, nodding vigorously. "Far as I can tell, anyway."

"Then…" Angus tugged at his lower lip. "This time-travel organization I'm going to found transports bodies."

Yorick nodded, puzzled.

"For that," Angus declared, "I need a time machine."

"Well, it might come in handy, yes."

"And I don't *have* a time machine."

"Yeah, well, I know you try to live on a budget…"

"So that's it." Angus spread his hands like a magician showing the coin had disappeared. "I can't found GRIPE."

Yorick frowned. "Why not?"

"Because I don't have a time machine, you nitwit!"

Yorick shrugged. "So invent one."

Angus sat looking at him for the space of three heartbeats. Then his lip curled. "Oh, sure! Just run on home and invent myself a time machine! What do you think I am, a wizard genius?"

Yorick nodded, and for a moment, his face held a look akin to worship.

Angus felt the temperature of his blood lower perceptibly.

Then the look was gone, and Yorick was smiling, nodding. "Yeah. That's right. Genius. What else could you call a man who's going to invent a time machine?"

"I'm not going to invent a time machine!" Angus snapped.

Yorick immediately turned wary. "Is… that another one of your— 'decisions'—Ang?"

Angus looked into the Neanderthal's eyes and shuddered. He believes it! He actually believes I can make a time machine!

Then he felt his native stubbornness rising again. He would not be buffaloed into…

"Well, it doesn't really matter," Yorick said hastily. "At least, not just yet. You don't really need a time machine to set up the organization; you've got non-physical time travel already. You can start recruiting agents and setting up the administrative machinery just with that."

Angus scowled; then his eyes lost focus, and a dreamy smile touched his face. "Y' know, you just might have something there! I could make a start that way, couldn't I?" He hitched forward in his chair. "Yeah! Set up... oh, call 'em sentries. Someone in each major historical period, to watch and report anything interesting—hey, the things you could find out that way!—and, uh, 'get in touch' once a week... Hell, why just the major periods? I could set up a network all down through history—even prehistory! As far back as the Neanderthals, at least, and..."

Yorick was grinning, nodding vigorously, eyes alight with enthusiasm.

Angus stared at him, his voice trailing off. Then his eyes narrowed and his jaw tightened. "No." He framed the word carefully. "N - O, No! I will not be conned into doing your scut work!"

Yorick almost seemed to deflate as his enthusiasm drained away. He closed his eyes, bowing his head and clenching his fists. Then he looked up at Angus with a woebegone smile. "Believe it or not, I'm not trying to con you into anything, Angus. You're going to do it of your own free will, or not at all."

Foreboding walked its fingers up Angus's back. He was beginning to realize that setting up GRIPE might be an inhuman responsibility, but it would also be work he could really put his heart into, the most satisfying labor he could possibly dream of—seeing Caesar's Rome, ancient Athens, solving the riddle of Atlantis, all the mysteries of history and prehistory. To watch Stonehenge being built...!

"Not because we want you to," Yorick murmured, "but because *you* want to. Setting up GRIPE, inventing the time machine—all of it."

Angus shivered with both excitement and pleasure.

Then he stiffened, staring through Yorick as a thought occurred to him. He pursed his lips, eyes unfocussed, nodding. "Listen—if I'm going to invent the time machine for GRIPE—who's going to invent one for SPITE? And VETO?"

"Why, you, of course." Yorick's eyebrows arched in surprise. "Only one time machine ever invented, and that was yours." He smiled. "You're the only man ever had a mind with just the right twist to be able to figure out how to ride through the dimensions."

Angus glared, then closed his eyes, shook his head violently. "No. No, I won't believe that. Me, give my invention to two organizations that've been trying to wipe me out since before I was born? No!" He glared at Yorick. "Crazy I may be, but not insane!"

"You're not," Yorick assured him, "and you won't be. Of course you wouldn't give them your time machine. But that doesn't mean they won't get it."

"They're going to steal it?" Angus clamped his jaw, slammed his fist on the table. "I'll sue them for patent infringement!"

"No patent." Yorick spread his hands. "You won't dare patent it, Ang. Anybody could get the plans then. That'd be putting it up for grabs."

"A detail." Angus waved it away. "I invented it, I've got the patent rights! They can't steal my machine!"

"They're going to," Yorick sang, grinning.

Angus stared, appalled, aggrieved, wounded to the core. "Why, the bastards! The inchronometrable bastards!"

Yorick's eyes danced. "Want to do something about it?"

"Damn right I do!" Angus shot to his feet, leveled a shaking forefinger at Yorick. "They're not going to get away with it. Oh, no. Not my time machine. I'll slam 'em down so hard they won't even know they've been buried!" He spun about and headed for the door, limping fast.

Yorick was right at his shoulder, grinning like a keyboard. "Kind of gripes you?"

"Damn right it does!" Angus lashed out at the doorway as he passed through. "Where do those bastards get off, thinking they can steal my damn time machine? And I haven't even invented it yet!"

Yorick escorted Angus home against his protests that he was perfectly safe (which Yorick doubted—and, for that matter, so did Angus). When they arrived at Angus's apartment, Yorick insisted on giving the room a thorough once-over, agreeing all the while that the search was ridiculous. He gave the room a clean bill of health, bade Angus a cheerful good-night, and left.

The door closed. Angus spent the first few minutes cursing steadily. Then, mollified but still disgruntled, he sat down at his desk with pencil and paper to try to figure out what was going on. He cast his mind back over everything Yorick had said, decided he couldn't really comprehend it, and let his mind wander, hoping for random correlations.

They came, but they weren't quite what he had anticipated.

Five minutes later, he laid down his pencil and looked at the paper before him. He had sketched out the basic organizational structure for GRIPE.

Exasperated with himself, he crumpled the sheet and threw it into the wastebasket, hard.

Then he frowned, cocking his head to the side, fought a short interior battle, gave in, and pulled the paper back out. It was a fun thing to fool around with...

He smoothed the paper and bent over it with a happy smile.

Then he frowned. No, not right at all; too long a chain from the general to the privates. All right, so maybe the low man couldn't be in direct, constant touch with the head honcho—but they could at least see each other occasionally…

He scowled, chewing on his lower lip as he mentally rearranged things. Two intermediate bosses, say, or maybe only one. Yeah, only generals, captains, and privates, and all the captains in touch with the general. Make for a busy general, but…

He shook his head, confused. He needed to get back to basics. He yanked open a file drawer and rooted around for the notes he'd made for the way InterContinental ought to be run…

Then he froze, staring at the papers.

Carefully, he took his hands from the drawer and studied what he saw. They were there, all right, his papers, in their usual random, junkheap collection, and in the same order, or lack thereof—but there was something wrong about it. It was a junkheap, all right, but it wasn't *his* junkheap! There are styles in the stacking of junk, as in everything else, and this just wasn't Angus's style. He couldn't have said why, but it wasn't.

He frowned and very carefully proceeded to go through the stack, paper by paper, very much on the watch for anything missing.

Nothing.

His eyes glittered for a moment, his jaw tightening, as he stared down into the drawer. Then he slammed it shut and yanked his spiral-bound journal from the stack of books on his desk. He opened it, leafed through it impatiently, page by page…

And froze, staring.

The page where he'd written down his random thoughts about his mental time-trip and his visit with Alasper was gone.

He stared at the shreds of paper that showed where the page was missing, stared unbelieving.

Then he frowned. It didn't make sense—if SPITE, or VETO, or whoever it was who had stolen that page wanted the information, why hadn't they just photographed it and left it in the book? Why take it away and run the risk of raising his suspicions?

Obviously because they didn't want him to have the information on that page.

For a moment, his lips twisted with contempt. The fools! Could they really believe there was even a chance he didn't have that information locked safe in his memory?

Then he frowned, nodded slowly. It was a good try and just might have worked. If he hadn't talked to Yorick that day, the next time he went looking for that page to refresh his memory about the time-trip, he wouldn't have been able to find it. And he would have been exasperated, angry, paranoid—and secretly relieved. He'd half wanted to believe it was all a dream, anyway. So he probably would have decided just that—or, being usually objective and not all that paranoid, he would have decided he'd just ripped the page out and thrown it away himself, and had forgotten about it (again, because he secretly wanted to). And, quite possibly, he would never have thought seriously about time-travel again.

It was possible. And, now that he thought about it, maybe not all that improbable.

He frowned, nodded slowly. Things were beginning to happen fast, now. Fleetingly, he wondered how many times they could try to kill him in one day...

He jerked bolt-upright in his chair. If they were trying to assassinate him, he was a fool to stay in this room. They might have something planted in here!

He relaxed again; Yorick had searched.

But could Yorick have missed something? After all, at this stage in his career, he was still a very young agent.

Angus bolted from the room like a flushed pheasant and hurried for the phone at the end of the hall. He leafed though the directory frantically; nothing under "Yorick."

But wait a minute. Was "Yorick" his real name? No, now that be thought or it—there had been another name on the big lug's nametag— Trawl? Tall? Thall!

Momentarily, he frowned, wondering at the name...

He shrugged, found the "T's." Yorick had to get over here fast; Angus was going to need protection now, and...

He stopped abruptly. His head came up slowly; he glared at his own reflection in the cracked mirror that hung over the phone. First thing he knew, he'd be asking Yorick to taste his food for him and maybe give him his bottle and make sure the formula was warmed to the right temperature...

He slammed the phone book down, disgusted with himself. He'd be blasted if he was going to hide behind anybody! Even... he swallowed nervously... when it was necessary!

A clammy feeling in the pit of his belly informed him that it probably was necessary—very.

He turned, growling, and limped down the stairs. If he died, he died— but while he lived, he'd live his own man! No hiding. None.

Besides, he reminded himself as he went out the door and down the front steps, he probably wasn't in any *physical* danger here; huge organizations didn't form elaborate conspiracies to bump off one insignificant cripple.

Let's see, what had Yorick said his address was? 130 East Liberty, that was it.

Elaborate conspiracies, against him, Angus McAran, of whom no one had ever heard? Ridiculous! He was definitely letting his paranoia get out of hand.

He stepped off the curb—and heard a sudden swelling roar. Paranoia took over; he lurched to his right, stumbled, tripped, and fell, kicking wildly to try to regain his balance. The roar filled the world; tires screeched, then the roar was fading into the distance.

Pain stabbed through his ankle, and he cursed; another sprain! Scarcely the first time it had happened.

But why had that car hurtled straight at him?

Imagination, he told himself angrily—just a drunken driver pulling too hard on the wheel and probably shocked and horrified to see someone in his headlights. He had probably pulled over now, and was shaking in his seat, afraid to come back and look to make sure his potential victim was still only potential. Angus used the anger to push himself to his knees, gritting his teeth against the pain, grabbed hold of a passing tree, and pulled himself to his feet. Bracing himself against the trunk, he lifted his right foot carefully, flexed it gingerly, then the knee, then tested the whole leg. It hurt like sunfire, but it moved just fine, nothing broken...

His shoe.

There, the heel was gone, torn away—and there was a gouge out of what remained of the three-inch sole.

He sighed, collapsing against the bark of the tree, thanking whatever Fates there were that had gifted him with a short right leg. If that had been his foot down there...

He shook off the mood, clamped his jaw, and turned his head from side to side, reorienting himself. Let's see... that way. East Liberty. Yorick's apartment. He pulled himself together and limped away. Maybe hiding behind Yorick wouldn't be such a bad idea, after all...

By the time he'd reached 130 East Liberty, he had, of course, changed his mind again. He was his own man and was going to stay that way, damn it! He wasn't about to hide behind anybody, least of all Yorick!

Still, he needed somebody to talk to, and on this particular subject, there was only one person available.

He found Apartment Four, knocked. A muffled bellow answered, "Just a minute!" Then the door swung in, and Yorick broke into a grin. "Ang! Good to see y'! What's new?"

"Murder," Angus rasped. "Somebody just tried to kill me!"

Yorick looked sympathetic. "Gets to be a drag after a while, doesn't it?"

Angus stared.

Then he found his voice. "Aren't you—a little concerned?"

"Oh, yeah, sure, of course."

"You sure as hell don't look it!"

Yorick shrugged. "You get used to it. Besides, you're alive, aren't you?"

Angus grunted surly agreement.

" 'Course, I do wish I'd been around." Yorick's lower lip stuck out. "I mean, all you had to do was call, Ang. I'd've been over to escort you in…"

"No!" Angus snapped.

"See?" Yorick spread his hands. "What can I do?"

Angus glared a moment, then lowered his head, nodding, mouth twisting. "Yeah. All right." His head came up. "But what you *can* do is listen!"

"Talk away." Yorick stepped back, opening the door wider. "I've got all night and a big ear."

Angus stumped in, growling under his breath. He looked around. Three rooms. Small, but two more than he had. "Do pretty well by yourself, don't you?"

"This?" Yorick choked on a laugh. "You call this 'good'?"

"Not bad at all, compared to my one room."

Yorick grinned. "Whatsa matter? You figure the head and founder of the organization oughta have better accommodations than a mere agent?"

"My agents aren't ever going to be 'mere'!" Angus's voice crackled.

Yorick raised his eyebrows; his mouth widened in a delighted smile.

Angus's face froze.

Then his eyes narrowed. "That doesn't mean I'm committed yet. I'll set up your organization, but that's all."

"Sure, Ang," Yorick said brightly. "That's why they tried to kill you tonight." Then quickly, because Angus's face was darkening and his mouth opening: "You didn't answer my question."

Angus looked scrambled a moment, then remembered the question. "Oh. Should I be living better then you? Answer: No. But I oughta be living at least as well, shouldn't I?"

"Sure." Yorick sauntered over to the desk with a nostalgic half-smile, murmuring, "Ah, the idealism of the early days…" He pulled open a drawer. "I've got a checkbook on the local GRIPE account right here—one of our cover corporations, *Research Undertaken Regardless, Inc.* How much y' want? Couple thousand?"

Angus blinked. He swallowed. He realized he was shivering. So he got angry. "No!"

"Didn't think you would," Yorick said cheerfully, turning back to him. "So…" He shrugged.

"I've got plenty of money! I just don't want to spend it!" Angus glared.

Yorick smiled blithely.

"Oh, hell!" Angus threw himself into an armchair, leaned his forehead into one hand.

Yorick shrugged. "So what can I do?"

"Offer me a drink," Angus said, disgusted. "Then listen."

"Coming right up!" Yorick hustled into the kitchen, came back minute later with a large tumblerful.

"Thanks." Angus took a sip, choked, eyes bulging, and heaved up a huge, racking cough.

Yorick raised his eyebrows. "Don't take bourbon straight?"

"Yeah, yeah, but I'm not used to *good* whiskey." Angus mopped at his eyes, then stilled. His head snapped up, eyes narrowed, pinioning Yorick. "How'd you know I took straight bourbon?"

Yorick opened his mouth…

"No!" Angus's hands shot up, palm out, to shield his face. He hunched down behind them. "On second thought, don't answer that." He had a notion he didn't want to hear the answer.

Besides, he already knew it. Yorick had learned it from Angus's older self.

Well, there was one consolation: at least he'd be able to afford good bourbon.

Yorick shrugged, folded into the other armchair, took a belt of his own drink. "What's on your mind?"

Angus hunched forward, elbows on his knees. "Somebody went through my papers while I was gone."

The room was very quite for a moment. Then Yorick said, "Anything missing?"

"Yeah." Angus looked up, the corners of his mouth tight. "My notes on my time-trip."

"Mm." Yorick's brows knit. "So they know the ball is rolling…"

Then his face cleared; he shrugged. "Well, we were pretty sure they knew that by this time, anyway. I mean, you're not exactly famous in the far future, Ang—your older se… ah, GRIPE… doesn't want you publicized—but SPITE did manage to get someone to do a biography of you."

"Of me?" For a moment, Angus's face was cherubic in its delight.

Then it tightened, eyes narrowed. "Wait a minute. That means SPITE and VETO know everything about me."

"No, only what they can glean from the public records." Yorick pulled out a stogie. "Which isn't much."

"Oh?" Angus raised an eyebrow. "Keep secrets pretty well, do you?"

Yorick looked up from lighting his cigar to nod, his eyes spearing Angus with accusation through the smoke.

Angus tried to glare back for a moment, then looked away, tasting gall. "All right, so I'm not so good on security! But—look, how was I supposed to know I had any secrets to keep!" His eyes snapped back to Yorick, returning the accusation.

Yorick sighed, resigned, and slumped back in his chair, eyeing his cigar ruefully. "Every now and then, Ang, I find it in me to wish you were just a little more paranoid... Well, it's just as well for the world that you're not, I suppose..."

Angus frowned. "How?"

" 'How' what?"

"How's it good for the world that I'm not more paranoid?" Angus demanded.

Yorick's frown turned quizzical. "Pretty obvious, isn't it? I mean, if you were really paranoid, you'd have a lust for power, and with a thing like time travel at your disposal..."

Angus stared in horror. Then he found his voice. "Ye gods!" He swallowed. "You... you don't think I'd..."

"No, of course not." For a moment, there was something almost fond in Yorick's look—but only for a moment. "For which, all your enemies, and all your friends, give a unanimous cheer."

"All?" Angus looked a little befuddled. "But I don't have any. Up until today..." His voice trailed off; he avoided Yorick's gaze.

Yorick grinned and puffed on his cigar.

Friends! Angus thought. *Lord!*

He shook himself, coming back to the matter at hand. "So. I'm going to have to be more—well, let's say security-conscious."

"Suspicious," Yorick said helpfully.

"Cautious," Angus snapped. "I've got to be more cautious. 'Cause if I'm going to have friends, I'm going to have enemies, too."

"Lots," Yorick said with massive conviction. "I don't happen to know whether or not you're ever going to meet any of them on a personal basis—but you'll be meeting them quite often on, shall we say, a professional level."

"Murder attempts," Angus translated. "And already, they hate me. They hated me before I was born."

"And tried to kill you in the womb." Yorick's eyes were hard. "Radiation—and a few esoteric substances in your mother's food..."

Angus stared.

Then his jaw set and his face turned into cold mayhem. "The bastards! The son-of-a-bitching..."

"It's done." Yorick cut him off, his face grave. "It's done and over with. I don't know all the details, but I do know that whatever they did was why you came out deformed." He smiled with bitter humor. "They found out they couldn't get her with 'accidents' or even guns, 'cause we always had somebody or three protecting her—without her knowing, of course. But we couldn't analyze everything she ate beforehand; we had to make do by making sure our doctors always got there in time. So you and your mother both came out alive—but 'alive' was the best we could do."

Angus smiled sardonically, massaging his right leg. "They outsmarted themselves. If it wasn't for this three-inch sole, that hit-and-run would have broken my leg—and maybe killed me, with physical shock."

Yorick's eyes flicked down to Angus's shoe. He nodded approvingly. "Took quite a gouge out of it, didn't they? Well—the best-laid plans, Ang, the best-laid plans."

Abruptly, he covered his eyes with his palm. "Ang... just a little paranoia, Ang. That's all I'm asking."

"Oh, don't worry." Angus's voice was silk. "I intend to be very careful indeed—and very suspicious. I'm feeling it already." He rubbed his leg, a slight smile on his lips.

Yorick grinned, relieved. "Great! What're you going to do about it?"

"First off..." Angus pursed his lips, checking the thoughts before he put words to them. "I think you and I had better become roommates."

Yorick nodded judiciously. "Not bad; we can pool our funds and get a bigger place—and I can at least make sure things stay safe indoors... I'll walk at your left shoulder any time you go anywhere—if you want, Ang."

"Uh, thanks, but..." Angus felt a little embarrassed at such devotion. Also a little paranoid; not being used to having friends, he felt a sort of emotional claustrophobia. "No, I don't think I want to go that far." He frowned suddenly. "I take it back—we do need to. But I need, even more, for you not to be my watchdog... Uh, it wouldn't hurt for you to teach me a few tricks about, uh, how to stay alive, though."

"Gladly, gladly," Yorick said, nodding. "What else do we do? How about an inch-thick armor-plate door?"

"Uh, that's going a little far. But a burglar alarm, I could go along with. Personal safety, though, I'm not going to sweat all that much."

Yorick looked sour. "I was afraid of that. All right." He cocked an eyebrow. "What *are* you going to sweat?"

"Papers," Angus answered. "And machinery, when—and *if*—I invent that time machine."

"Uh..." Yorick's lips turned inward. " 'Scuse me, Ang, but—'if'?"

Angus shrugged impatiently. "The only thing I've decided on is setting up GRIPE. As to the time machine—well, I don't even know if I *can* invent it."

Yorick grinned. "Oh, you can invent it, all right. You can."

"I wish I had as much confidence in me as you do," Angus grumbled.

He made an abrupt chopping motion. "That's aside. The point is, if I *do* invent it, we're going to need a very safe place to hide it."

"Fine." Yorick spread his hands. "Where?"

Angus smiled with sarcasm. "How about a mile deep in rock, with no doors. That *might* be safe enough." He frowned suddenly, his eyes losing focus.

Yorick watched, grinning around his cigar.

"Y'know," Angus said slowly, "that's not such a bad idea."

"Fine." There was a hungry glint in Yorick's eye. "Where?"

Angus snapped back to reality. "How the hell should I know! Besides, it's impossible."

"Not so impossible as you might…" Yorick broke off, his eyes losing focus.

Angus watched him with a jaundiced eye.

"So *that's* where it is!" Yorick breathed.

"Where what is?" Angus was wary.

"GRIPE Headquarters." Yorick's eyes focused again, on Angus. "See, I had to take a few courses to get my degree, and I took Anthro, of course, and a couple geology courses, since I got this thing about rocks—used to chip flints in my boyhood…" Wistfulness and nostalgia rippled across his face and were gone. "Anyway, we took this field trip that summer, to the Grand Teton Mountains in the Rockies, Anthro department was excavating an old Folsom People site—and I took a hike with a sonar unit and a seismograph and some blasting caps, one afternoon. Free time, you understand; I didn't have to report on it to anybody, and I didn't, they'd have thought I was bananas."

"Oh?" Angus's eyes kindled. "What'd you find?"

"Well…" Yorick pursed his lips, blew out a long jet of smoke. "According to the machines, there's this huge cavern there, about two hundred feet in diameter, a half-mile down into bedrock, and it's a perfect sphere."

"What!!?!"

Yorick shrugged. "All's I know's what I read on the graph papers— and that's what they said. Didn't believe it at the time myself, so I didn't tell anybody—but I had the instruments checked, and they were perfectly kosher."

Angus looked dubious. "How?"

"Good question." Yorick sucked on his lower lips, gazing at the wall. "All I can figure is, a huge gas bubble formed when the mountain was molten—only the mountain cooled around it faster than the gas could get out. Better go in with gas masks, the first time or two, till the air's been exchanged."

Angus frowned, puzzled.

"So," Yorick concluded, "there's this huge spherical cavern in there, without an entrance or exit." He grinned triumphantly. *"There's* your hideout!"

Angus looked skeptical. "If this's where GRIPE headquarters is, how come you didn't know about it?"

Yorick threw up his hands in disgust. "Of all the…! Look, Ang, you may not be much on security, but your friends fortunately are! And you know the old principle, 'what you don't know, you can't tell.' So only Doc—pardon, your older self—knows where HQ is. Well…" He frowned, suddenly thoughtful. "My older self must know, too, come to think of it. But they're the only ones—except you and me, now, of course. And, since we're really them…"

"Uh, never mind," Angus said quickly. He had a notion time paradoxes were better taken in light doses. "I'll take your word for it—but I have one small question."

"Shoot." Yorick sat back, puffing his stogie, steepling his fingers.

"How—do we get—in and out? Since this cavern doesn't have any doors?"

Yorick frowned. "By using the time machine, of course."

"Great!" Angus rolled his eyes up, exasperated. "Now all I have to do is invent it!"

"Sure." Yorick grinned, leaning forward. "See, the thing functions as a matter transmitter as well as a time machine—since it goes through the fifth dimension and it's transmitting matter from past to future anyway, all you have to do is give it spatial co-ordinates, and you've got a matter transmitter. Set the time co-ordinates for 'present,' and you've got *only* a matter transmitter. So matter-transmitting is sort of a bonus, a secondary characteristic of… uh… Ang?"

Angus's eyes had glazed; his face glowed with a strange sort of exhilaration. "Matter transmitter," he muttered. "Now *that*… Say, y'know, it might…"

Yorick said, very carefully, "You, uh—got an idea?"

"Sure." Angus nodded, still in rapture. "A time machine, no. How're you going to propel something through time? How're you going to make that much power in a portable power source? No way."

Yorick nodded, eyes glowing.

"But a matter transmitter's easy!" Angus turned back to Yorick, grinning. "You only have to go into the fourth dimension, not the fifth—and you can bounce the object you're transmitting off the interface, the… Well, call it the chronocline, the difference in energy levels between the dimensions, so you can just shoot it in like a bank shot on a pool table, and…"

Yorick nodded eagerly, grinning open-mouthed.

"And that's it!" Angus crowed, catching Yorick's enthusiasm. "All you do is slide your three-dimensional matter into the chronocline, and you… Well, it's like you just—shoot it in at the right angle, and, well, uh… Angle or angles? Uh… complex of angles, with your basic fourth-dimensional matrix… Uh, matrices? Anyway, you… What the hell!" He slammed to his feet. "You got a couple of flashlight batteries and some bell wire?"

KLEIN COILS

PART II

A frantic hour and a half later, they stood gazing down with exhausted satisfaction at what had been Yorick's breadboard. It was now a nightmare jumble of bell wire, resistors, and vacuum tubes (from an innocent, unwitting radio that now lay nearby, ravished), a rheostat (also from the radio), a variable condenser (there wasn't much left of the radio), a transformer (from a poor, defenseless doorbell that had never done anyone any harm), and a small, circular platform (improvised out of a captive quarter, in defiance of Federal law) on three short, one-inch legs (formerly paper clips). At the bottom of Washington's neck and in front of his nose lay two sinister, hand-wound coils, intersecting at Washington's ear to form a ninety-degree angle. Directly above the quarter hung a third coil.

There was something strange about those coils. Only a warped mind could have conceived such convolutions—or a mind that had spent too long looking at Klein bottles.

"Great," Yorick breathed, from the heights of euphoria. "It looks just great, Ang."

"Gee, thanks." Angus had a foolish grin and a modest blush. "It ain't much, really, but I like it, and it's kinda… well…" His voice trailed off.

Yorick nodded. "It sure is." He eyed Angus out of the corner of his eye. "What does it do?"

"Well, uh…" Angus pointed at the three coils. "You know how a magnetic field intersecting a piece of wire causes a flow of current, right?"

"Uh…"

"Right. Induction. And how an energized coil can shoot a piece of iron along the axis of the core, right?"

"Yeah, but…"

"A solenoid. Sure. Now, the trick is to get the whole atom moving by induction, instead of just the electrons, so it'll act like a solenoid, but for things that aren't made out of iron."

Yorick lifted a skeptical eyebrow. "It makes a nice analogy, Ang. But is this story-time?"

Angus shrugged. "That's as well as I can explain it. Each coil is wound so that it produces a field that's something like electricity and something like magnetism, and more like something else there isn't a word for—and when you turn on the current, it propels whatever's on the stage—excuse me, the quarter—along the axis of the coil."

"Axis?" Yorick's eyes crossed. "Of those coils?"

"Yeah, well, that's the other thing about those coils," Angus admitted.

"In three-dimensional terms, they have about as much of an axis as an oval has a center. But in four-dimensional terms, each coil has one nice straight axis."

"I'll take your word for it." Yorick eyed the coils as though they were tarantulas. "Myself, I never did care to really watch what was happening when I was personality-projection-time-traveling. Matter of fact, I'm beginning to understand why I never wanted a look at the innards of a time machine… Okay, Ang, so each coil has an axis, and it'll shoot any chunk of matter along that axis. Then what?"

Angus shrugged. "Anything at the point of intersection of the three fields—that's George's ear, there—gets projected at a right angle to all three dimensions…"

"Into the fourth dimension!" Yorick hissed, staring at the quarter with eyes just as round.

"Like a pea out of a beanshooter," Angus said happily. "And however much power you shoot it with determines how far it goes, and the variable condenser determines the complex of angles—well, hell, the vector—at which it strikes the choroncline, so that determines which direction you're shooting it, and…"

"Huh?" Yorick's head looped the loop. "Whoa, Ang! Back it up, there! How's the variable condenser give it direction?"

"Well… it…" Angus's hands flapped uselessly. "Well, it sort of… it… moves it around, through—no, that's a straight line, really, in four-dimensional space, and it… uh… no… Damn it, don't ask me how it works! How should I know? I just built the blasted thing!"

"Yeah, that's a good point." Yorick nodded, frowning. "We'll leave the explanations to the theoretical physicists."

"Yeah. I've done my part." Angus turned away, jammed the plug into the wall.

"But how'd you know how to make it do what it does, Ang?"

"Because I've been there."

"And you were watching the scenery." Yorick shuddered. "I never dared; it would've warped my mind."

"Yeah, well, that's the advantage to having a warped way of thinking to being with," Angus said. "The scenery couldn't have done mine much damage."

"There is a certain irregular contour to your thoughts," Yorick admitted. "So you just watched what happened. Should work. I mean…"

"Yeah." Angus turned to the kitchen cabinets. "Once you've ridden in a wagon, you've got the general idea of hooking up a horse to something on wheels."

"If you were watching the horse and looking down at the wagon, instead of keeping your eyes tight shut... uh... Ang? Whatcha looking for?"

"Sugar," Angus said. "Got any cubes?"

"It is about time for a coffee break." Yorick opened a door and took out a box.

"Thanks, I'll take mine plain." Angus took the box and shook out a cube.

Yorick frowned. "Didn't know you had a sweet tooth."

"I don't." Angus turned back and placed the cube on the quarter.

Yorick stared. "Pardon me for asking, but what are you doing?"

"Setting up the first shot." Angus checked to make sure the little white cube was in the precise center of the silver circle.

A slow delighted grin spread over Yorick's face.

"Shall we try it?"

"Yeah, why not?" Angus grinned back. He nudged the rheostat, just barely opening it. "Only a little power, this time, a smidgen..."

The transformer hummed.

The cube disappeared.

They both stared pop-eyed at the quarter, not quite able to believe it.

Yorick recovered first. "Quick! Which way did it go?"

"Uh... uh..." Angus glanced at the variable condenser; it was closed tight. "North," he muttered sheepishly. He'd forgotten to set it.

"North! North..." Yorick pivoted in a circle, right arm straight out from the shoulder. "Let's see, the sun rises at the kitchen window, so that's east... The living room! North!"

As one, they leaped for the doorway, craned their necks around the jamb.

Nothing.

"Uh... how far'd y' throw it, Ang?"

"Hell, how should I know? We'll have to calibrate the damn thing by guess and by golly."

Yorick's mouth tightened; he shook his head with conviction. "No sugar cube, Ang."

"None." Angus sagged.

Then he pulled himself together. "Well, maybe a little power went a long way. Let's check the front lawn." He lifted his head, squared his shoulders. "Come on!" He put his best foot forward, and...

Something crunched under his heel.

Angus froze.

Slowly, he turned his head toward Yorick.

Grins spread over both their faces.

Then Angus was hopping away and Yorick was on his knees, hands scrabbling over the floor, and Angus was shouting, "Was that it? Is it sugar? Do we gotta sweep the floor? Are we gonna have cockroaches?"

Yorick licked his forefinger, touched it to the linoleum, then touched it to his tongue and lifted his head with a look of insane glee.

"Sugar!" they both roared together.

Then, for five minutes, the apartment rocked with the whooping and stomping of a victory dance.

They spent the rest of the night calibrating the matter transmitter, the rheostat for distance and the variable condenser for direction, until Angus could put a half-inch cube of sugar precisely on target anywhere within the apartment, the cube obediently disappearing from the quarter and reappearing where it was wanted, three tries out of three, every time.

Then (about four a.m.), they started experimenting with larger amounts of power, checking the range available with the current supplied by a doorbell transformer. Yorick went to a phone booth about two blocks away and called in. Angus bent over the breadboard with one hand on the rheostat and the other on the variable condenser, the phone cradled between ear and shoulder.

"Did I hit you?"

"Nope. Try again."

"Okay... We're gonna need more sugar cubes, Yorick."

"Don't worry about it, I know this all-night cafe..."

"Roger. Okay... There!"

"Where?"

"In your phone booth."

"Wanna bet?"

On the fifth try, Angus managed to place the cube on the palm of Yorick's hand. The Neanderthal came up with a whoop of joy that he must have dredged up whole and bodily out of his chertz-chipping childhood, and Angus was deaf in one ear for a half-hour afterward.

He did a few calculations while Yorick hiked to another phone booth halfway across town (fortunately, the caveman kept a slide rule in the house). Angus worked out a quick rule of thumb, and managed to put the sugar cube in Yorick's hand on the first try. Yorick's victory cry made a permanent dent in the diaphragm of the phone, but Angus had wisely laid the receiver half-way across the room before he pushed the button, so his auditory nerves were only slightly overloaded.

Sunrise saw Yorick standing in a neighboring town thirty miles away. Angus opened the rheostat full, pushed the button, and put the sugar cube in Yorick's s palm.

"First try," Yorick trumpeted over the phone.

"Aw, hell, it was easy," Angus muttered, a little embarrassed. And, to forestall further congratulations: "How about breakfast?"

In the next few weeks, Angus experimented blind. He found that the size of the coil had absolutely no relationship to its size or the payload. He beefed up the circuit for house current, ran a few calculations, and decided that the new heavy-duty model should have a range of four thousand miles. To test it out, he built a six-foot-square sign, rigged a jack brace to hold it upright, painted it black and, in flame-red letters on the black background:

**SINNERS, REPENT!
WHAT HAPPENED TO KRAKATOA
COULD HAPPEN TO YOU!**

He put in the huge poster in the focus of the three coils, set the controls for a remote destination, and pushed the button.

The next evening, Yorick came sauntering in chewing on his lower lip looking at a newspaper. "Funny thing here, Ang…"

Angus put down his book and looked up. "Oh? What?"

"Seems some nut put up a sign in the middle of Honolulu prophesying doom for the island."

"Yeah, well, y' know, mysticism's making a comeback."

" 'Course." Yorick sat down, lit a cigar. "Cops think somebody musta snuck in during the night and left it. But there's witnesses claim it wasn't there at midnight, or at three a.m., or at dawn, even."

"Don't say!"

"Do. And there's a coupla nut cases claim they saw the sign just appear outa thin air."

"They're all over the place these days."

"Guess so." Yorick knocked the ash off his cigar with exaggerated care. "Never know, though, Ang—might be some truth in what they say."

"Flying saucer," Angus offered. "Outa season."

Yorick nodded.

With the test phases done, Angus made up a clean workman-like version of the machine, destroyed the breadboard circuit, and built the new one into a cabinet four inches high, sixteen inches wide, and a foot deep. He used standard indicators on the front, so the whole thing looked like a do-it-yourself stereo radio. The camouflage seemed appropriate, so he built in an FM radio and stereo amplifier that was in no way connected with the matter transmitter (though it would have taken an engineer with a First Class FCC certificate to realize that) and wired the whole thing into his real stereo system.

The next week, Yorick took a short vacation and went to the Rockies, getting the exact co-ordinates for the subterranean cavern. It only took three days, counting travel time, but when he walked in the apartment door, Angus exploded, "What took you so damn long!"

"Easy, Ang." Yorick backed off warily. "Takes a little time to drive that far, y' know. I shaved it as close as I could and I'm dead on my feet, but still it takes time."

Angus swallowed as much of his pride as he could stomach, muttered an apology, and turned away to his bedroom.

He took the three coils out of his desk drawer, put one on the bed, one on the chair, hung the third from the light fixture, checked their focus, and plugged them into his "stereo." Angus set up the co-ordinates while Yorick strapped himself into a parachute (in case Angus was a little off on the settings), cradled a second matter-transmitter in his arms, and took his courage in his teeth. After all, Angus was still new to the game. "What happens if we figured wrong?"

"Don't worry, I built in a sort of radar that checks to make sure there's nothing in your destination zone before it lets you go through."

"A 'sort of' radar?"

"Four-dimensional," Angus explained.

"That still doesn't seem like much of a guarantee that I won't materialize inside solid rock."

"Relax," Angus said sourly. "A sphere three hundred feet in diameter—could I miss a target that large?"

Yorick swallowed heavily and said, "I'm trusting you, Ang."

Angus snarled and pushed the button. Yorick disappeared.

Then Angus let himself tremble, let his eyes blur.

He waited.

And waited.

And waited and waited and waited.

He'd worked through his fingernails and was down to the cuticle by the time Yorick reappeared. Angus stared, stupefied.

Yorick grinned.

"What took you so long!" Angus screamed. Then he threw his arms around the Neanderthal and hugged him like a brother. "Damnation! I thought I'd misfired!"

"Not a chance." Yorick waved a hand in deprecation. "Nothing to it. You put me in there two inches above floor level—perfect landing. But it took a while to set up the battery pack and hook it up—by the way, the batteries are probably drained just from that one shot. You better send through the generator."

"Huh...? Oh! Oh, yeah!" Angus yanked the small gasoline generator up onto a small table. He and Yorick manhandled the table into the focus of the three coils. Yorick stepped back; Angus pushed the button. The generator disappeared; so did the table.

Angus stared.

Then he blinked, looked up at Yorick. "Got a few bugs to iron out, yet... I take it the air was okay?"

"Iyuch!" Yorick's nose wrinkled. "Still a lotta sulfur dioxide in there, Ang—but I didn't need the gas mask. There was air enough coming through the machine, as long as I didn't get too far away from it."

"Hmm..." Angus tugged at his chin. "Looks like we'll have to leave the machine open a while, then, doesn't it?"

"Quite a while," Yorick agreed, "and rig a remote switch on the machine in the cavern, so we can shut it off from here. Otherwise the whole house'll stink like rotten eggs."

"Yeah." Angus frowned. "And sooner or later, we'll have to put in hydroponics beds, to keep the air fresh."

"Always wondered how we managed to have fresh vegetables." Yorick nodded, musing. "Well, that's for the future. For now, I better get back there and hook up that generator. See ya in a few minutes, Ang."

He sauntered into the focus and disappeared. Angus blinked.

He turned away trying to still a shudder. After all, it was a normal means of transportation, to Yorick...

And it kind of beat hitch-hiking.

The long-toothed cat growled in darkness. The stars were stabs of ice. Aachtuu turned from the glowing coal that would not flame and lifted his spear.

"Get out!" roared his father.

Aacthuu threw himself forward as the long-tooth sprang. His shoulder struck its chest, but its fangs sank into his back. He gasped and thrust with his spear, then thrust and heaved with his arms. The great claws flailed for his face and throat; he threw, and heard the body jar and snap. The cat screamed once before Aacthuu felt the welling, sticky warmth at his own throat, saw the meadows blur and fade.

The stars winked once in passing.

It was a few days before Angus managed to work up the nerve to step into the focus himself. When he did, he was amazed at how simple it was—a moment of dizziness, and there he was, standing in a pool of flashlight with darkness all around.

"Welcome to home, Ang!"

Angus turned, saw Yorick sitting at the kitchen table he'd brought through the day before, with a bottle or bourbon at his elbow and a cigar in his mouth.

Angus shuddered; it was pretty bad when the cigar was definitely an improvement. There was still a lot of sulfur dioxide in the air. He took a seat near Yorick to get within the noxious but bearable shield of cigar smoke. "So," he said softly, looking around at the darkness, "this is GRIPE headquarters."

"Will be, will be," Yorick said complacently.

He took a swig from the bottle. "Doesn't look like much now, I'll admit—but in ten years, this little hole'll be busier than Grand Central at rush hour."

Angus frowned, puzzled. "I thought most of the GRIPE personnel were going to be sentries, living in their own time."

"No way." Yorick waved expansively at the darkness. "This place'll be full of mobile time agents, Ang."

Angus's lips tightened. "*If* I invent the time machine!"

Yorick stilled. Slowly, he turned to Angus. "Still haven't decided on that?"

"How *can* I?" Angus snapped. "How can I even begin to? I don't even know how to build it yet!"

"As to that..." Yorick levered the top off a small cooler. "Time can work wonders, Ang." He poured some bourbon in a paper cup, mixed it with an ice cube, handed it to Angus. "But how about 'if'? *If* you figure out how to make a time machine—will you?"

"I don't know!" Angus barked. He shoved himself to his feet, began pacing.

Yorick fixed himself another drink, closed the cooler, and leaned back.

"The responsibility's too big," Angus growled.

"Do tell," Yorick murmured.

"Yes, damn it!" Angus took a long sip. "F'rinstance—this business about mobile agents. If we recruit a man as a time agent, take him out of his own age and place, what's going to happen to all the things he did, all the people he influenced, all the rest of his 'life'?"

Yorick nodded judiciously. "Might be pretty bad if you snagged, say, an eight-year-old kid who turned out to be Oliver Cromwell's grandfather. Then, no Oliver Cromwell. I admit, Charles I would probably be grateful— but how about the rest of England?"

"And all Charles II's illegitimate French children." Angus nodded glumly. "So we'd have to choose a man who's not going to have any effect on anybody, after the time we grab him. Which means..."

"...a dead man," Yorick finished. "Or a man who would have been dead, about thirty seconds after we grabbed him."

Angus nodded. "And if we're going to pull this time-style kidnapping without creating legends about evil trolls who steal children in broad daylight…"

"Or," Yorick interjected, "getting the New York City Police Force of 1892 rather worked up. And possibly getting Sherlock Holmes called across the Atlantic to chase our wild goose…"

Angus nodded. "So we've got to grab the kid while he's alone, and nobody's watching."

" 'Kid'?" Yorick lifted an eyebrow. "Why not an adult?"

Angus gave him a quick look of disgust. "Look, it's hard enough for *me* to get used to the idea of a time machine, and I'm supposed to be inventing it! The older they are, the harder it'll be for 'em to accept the concept without going bananas!"

"Hmm…" Yorick pursed his lips. "So—the younger we get 'em, the better. Which means…"

"That we're going to be running a home for the youthful and dead," Angus groaned. "Oh well, they matured fast, in the old days…" He suddenly stiffened, staring straight ahead. "Hey!"

"It's made out of grass," Yorick supplied helpfully.

Angus glared at him. "When I need bad punch lines, I can supply them myself. …Look, we'll need people who won't have any future life to affect other people, right?"

"Right." Yorick nodded. "That's the big thing—that your ideal time agent won't have had even the slightest affect on history after the time we grab him."

"Not to mention the time he dies." Angus smiled sourly. "He can't affect *any*body. Right?"

Yorick nodded, puzzled.

Angus's mouth worked. "How many parents do you know who aren't affected by a child's death?"

Yorick's face went into neutral. "I've heard of some. So we've gotta steal a kid that nobody cares about, huh?"

"An orphan," Angus growled.

"That'd be the best," Yorick agreed. "An eight-year-old kid with no living relatives. We oughta do real well if we scout around the edges of the Bubonic Plague."

Angus shuddered. "I hate to admit it, but you're probably right; the Black Death would be an excellent recruiting locus. A kid whose relatives are already dead, and who's just about to die himself… Then we wouldn't even be killing any scavengers that ate *him*, 'cause the only things that did were the worms in the mass graves, and the grass that grew out of them— and I don't think the worms and the grass would miss one small body all that much… Gak! Am I really saying this stuff?"

"You are," Yorick commiserated, "but I don't think it has to be all *that* morbid, Ang."

"Oh?" Angus gave him a jaundiced glare. "Got any better ideas?"

"Sure." Yorick knocked back the rest of his drink. "Say we took a hunter who was just about to be killed and eaten by a tiger…"

"We'd be depriving the tiger of dinner," Angus snapped, "and who knows? Maybe that tiger changed history."

"Yeah, he might've been Shere Khan," Yorick mused, "and if we caused him to die of starvation, what'd happen to Kipling's *Jungle Book*?"

"Just so," Angus grunted.

"But," Yorick demurred, "if the hunter was going to kill the tiger while the tiger was killing *him*…"

Angus stared.

"Who're we depriving then, Ang?" Yorick asked softly.

"Maybe some vultures," Angus muttered.

Yorick grimaced with impatience and disgust. "So leave 'em an equivalent mass of hamburger! And a plastic skeleton for any passersby to see, if you're really all that worried. But I don't think one vulture more or less is really gonna make all that much difference to history, Ang."

"Maybe not," Angus said thoughtfully, "but the plastic skeleton might not be such a bad idea… Oughta be *some* mortal remains, or we'll have a witch-hunt started on our account…"

Yorick shrugged. "Plenty of legends about elves stealing kids already, Ang. What's one more? Or less, for that matter. But sure, we can make up some good plastic bones if we have to. Cheaper than the real thing, come to think of it."

Angus was nodding faster and faster. "That might, just might, work! A kid, who dies out someplace alone, without witnesses, in such a way that he doesn't affect any other living beings… And the circumstances of his death exactly duplicated…" He froze a moment, then turned slowly to Yorick, glaring. "You knew all this already, didn't you?"

"Sure." Yorick spread his heads. "But you had to think it up, Ang. The circle has to start someplace. What would happen to those kids if you don't invent the time machine?"

"But what will happen to other people if I do?" Angus whispered.

Yorick waited.

"The military," Angus muttered. "Organized crime. What if they got hold of time machines? Or even matter transmitters?"

"Make sure they don't then," Yorick said quietly. "Security."

Angus gave an impatient twist of the head. "It always breaks down."

"Who's going to get in here *without* a matter transmitter?" Yorick asked. "No one can steal this secret, Ang."

"The machine," Angus muttered, "the one in the apartment."

"Keep it here," Yorick suggested. "A remote switch on the second machine. Press the button, and the first machine is right there before you."

"What if somebody finds the button?"

"Make it small enough to keep with you."

Angus's lips turned inward. "Agents. One of them's going to sell what he knows."

"Who'd believe him?"

Angus bowed his head.

Yorick sighed, turning away to take the pressure off Angus. "Somebody probably *will* sell out. SPITE and VETO had to get the machine somehow. But—the military? The Syndicate? The one's had too many cranks, the other knows too much about cons."

Angus nodded, slowly.

Yorick sat back. "That leaves SPITE and VETO—and we know they're going to get the machine. Maybe from your plans, maybe from their own inventors—we still don't know. Maybe we can't prevent them from getting it—but..." his eyes glittered "...we can make it damn tough on them when they do!"

Angus turned slowly to look at him. He nodded. "Yes. The time machine's mine. I'm going to invent it first—I've got a right to say who uses it and who doesn't—right, hell! A *duty!*" His fist slammed his thigh. "And anyone who pirates it..." His voice trailed off, but his face was very grim.

Their two gazes stayed locked a while, caveman and engineer, both with the same scrupled purpose—and nothing else.

Then Angus's gaze wavered; he looked down, turned away. "But... Yorick... there's a much easier, much more certain way to be sure they don't get the time machine."

Yorick closed his eyes, bowing his head in weariness, disgust, and temporary defeat.

"A much surer way," Angus murmured. "Don't invent it."

By the end of the week, using GRIPE's local bank account, they had set up a complete office in the cavern, with mahogany-veneer walls, carpeting, fluorescent lights, running water, and a coffeepot. There were also a desk, a chair, a typewriter, and a filing cabinet.

Angus liked it. It was one place where he felt he could really get away from it all.

For the rest of his life, he always intended to take a trip to the Grand Tetons by more conventional means, just to see what the mountain looked like from the outside; but somehow, he never got around to it.

With a real office (and a highly burglar-proof one), he was able to settle down to the long, slow grind of setting up the organization. He and Yorick had, of course, moved into more spacious quarters by this time—a huge old two-bedroom apartment, complete with rickety woodwork, crumbling plaster, plumbing problems, and cockroaches. But it wasn't too expensive (Angus still would not touch a penny of GRIPE's money for personal use, and wouldn't invade his own savings or investments) and had plenty of room.

Privately, Angus felt it could have been the size of a football field and still have been too small. He felt cramped by having a roommate—even though he could scarcely have asked for a more congenial one than Yorick. The stocky Neanderthal was always cheerful, always smiling, an excellent housekeeper and a good conversationalist.

It was driving Angus up a tree.

Not that he saw that much of Yorick. They both had to keep up the cover of their jobs—wouldn't do to have SPITE and VETO agents alerted by a huge and sudden change in their lifestyles—and Angus was putting in at least two hours of non-physical time travel (recruiting sentries) every night, and trying to keep up with his graduate studies. He didn't have much time for social life. Or sleep.

Yorick, for his part, worried about all the accidents that could happen on Angus's way to work when he was groggy from lack of sleep—and the cranky one wouldn't think of hiring a limo. Nonetheless, Yorick kept smiling.

Just one frown, *Angus thought,* just one…

The two hours' time travel each night were fascinating, at first. Angus spent the first week just having conversations with Alasper (the older Yorick). He kept trying to pump the old caveman for information about GRIPE and the details of his own future, but if there was ever a man who was capable of being garrulous and close-mouthed at the same time, it was Yorick, no matter what his age.

When Angus realized he was beginning to intensify his inferiority complex, due to being consistently outsmarted by a Neanderthal, he skipped ahead to the week before Alasper's retirement and asked the senior agent to introduce him to a promising young candidate for sentry work. The candidate in question already knew all about GRIPE and was awed and delighted to meet "Dr. McAran" first hand. He was so effusive in his protestations of loyal service that Angus cut the interview as short as possible and pulled out. Then he skipped ahead to the week before the candidate's retirement and had him introduce Angus to another candidate. The youngster's name was Balank; he was already thoroughly indoctrinated, and demonstrated even more of a puppy-dog worshipfulness than his predecessor. Angus lingered just long enough for a jury-rigged swearing-in ceremony, then pulled out, fast.

It was beginning to get him down.

And so things went all up the time line. Angus's mood was not improved by the constant references to his older self, nor by the tone of awe that went with them.

Consequently, it was very refreshing to occasionally chance across a candidate (anyone who happened to be in the time trance was fair game) that had never heard of GRIPE.

It did happen occasionally. There were a few dots of light on the time line that had not been contacted before Angus encountered them— apparently the time trance did happen accidentally, on occasion. For instance, Kiyu.

Kiyu was the oldest member of GRIPE—oldest in that he was the furthest back in prehistory, circa 200,000 B.C.. In years, he was sixteen. He had deliberately eaten some mushrooms that the tribe's shaman had definitely warned everyone to avoid, and was squatting in front of the fire trying to figure out where the flames came from when Angus stepped into his mind and informed him that flames resulted from the rapid oxidation of the carbon in the wood.

Kiyu almost collapsed from shock and fright. He started making gibbering noises about a visitation from the gods (with a sub-text of "Why did it have to happen to me?"). It took Angus a while to calm him down and disabuse him of the notion (more or less). But once he got the basic concepts across, Kiyu swore unswerving loyalty for the rest of his life and, moreover, promised that his son (who was then three months old) would swear similar loyalty for the rest of *his* life—and his son too, and his son's son, and so on—at which point Angus cut him off and informed him that it would be up to each son as to whether or not he wanted to enlist in GRIPE.

After a rapid swearing-in ceremony (Angus was beginning to get pretty good at it: he scarcely had to think about the words any more), Angus left, rather quickly, as Kiyu was making a fervent promise to tune in every week, on the dot.

It was a little depressing. Better than being told his older self had already been there, though... Still, such accidental trances were few, and far between on the time-line.

After that first contact with Kiyu, all Angus had to do was go up the time line swearing in successors as they appeared. Kiyu was a homebody, staying pretty close to his cave near Heidelberg, but his son Lenhrang (who, as it turned out, did want to enlist in GRIPE) was a wanderer who, for thirty years of his life, rambled all over Europe, Asia Minor, and a sizeable chunk of Africa, narrowly escaping sudden death several times, and constantly enlisting new GRIPE sentries (all of whom Angus had to swear in; the personal oath was already a tradition). At the age at fifty, Lenhrang returned to Heidelberg and settled down, leaving Angus with sentries spread over most of the human-inhabited Old World, except East and Southern Asia.

However, Angus had been busy there, too. Thanks to the each-one-recruit-two plan, there were several hundred sentries spread over the Eastern Hemisphere by the time of the Bering Straits migration (Angus was processing recruits at the rate of thirty a night) and, of course, three of the migrants were GRIPE agents.

Then he had to start processing recruits from the New World, too, and… Well, it was getting to be a bit of a grind.

A lot of things had become a grind. Angus threw himself into his studies and his job at ICBM with the fervor of the hunted. Yorick sat in the living room, smiling, smoking his cigars and drinking his beer—and worrying.

He was very worried. He knew that the routine work had to be done, and that only Angus could do it at this stage; but he also knew that routine work always made Angus McAran depressed. He'd had ample time to learn it—he'd known Doc (the older Angus) for a long time. And Doc Angus had always showed his depression by becoming even more grouchy and irritable.

But this was a new Angus, and a new kind of depression. Deeper, maybe. Withdrawn.

Then one evening, when Angus finally relented and agreed to shovel in some food no matter how hungry he wasn't, and Yorick was feverishly trying to be amusing, he said something about the unreliability of VETO agents.

Angus looked up with a frown. "Seems to me I can always depend on them to try to kill me."

"Yes, but they choose their own times," Yorick said. "We can't be sure exactly when they're going to take a shot at you. That's why we have to shadow you night and…" He broke off at the look of shock in Angus's face. "Ang… what's the matter, man?"

"The bomb in the table," Angus said in a hoarse voice.

Yorick froze for a tell-tale second, then relaxed way too much. "Yeah, it was just good luck I was there."

"Good luck, hell!" Angus thrust himself to his feet. "Very opportune, don't you think? A bomb ticking away right next to me when you were trying to persuade me that enemy agents were trying to kill me!"

"These things happen all the time," Yorick said desperately.

"Yeah, but not with such excellent timing!" Angus threw down his napkin. "You planted that bomb yourself!"

"Look, SPITE and VETO really *are* trying to murder you…"

"Oh, I believe it! They most definitely are, and they don't particularly care who else gets killed in the process! But you couldn't have depended on their making a murder attempt at just the right moment to help convince me!" Angus turned on his heel and stalked out.

"No, Ang, wait…"

But the only answer was the slam of the door.

TIME MACHINE

PART III

Down the sidewalk Angus went, through the old limestone columns that served as a gateway into the park. He was so deeply immersed in brooding anger that he didn't even remember the park could be dangerous at night.

His mind roamed, wisps of thought coming through the dark haze, brushing here, touching there. He probably could've followed a line of thought if he had wanted to, but he didn't.

He walked, and he thought, and thought, and thought, and walked, and walked…

Something in the back of his mind nagged, telling him: *This is dangerous. Don't do it. Go home; get Yorick to walk with you. It's dangerous. Don't walk…* but only at the back of his mind. He was accustomed to it, now—and suddenly wasn't sure that he could trust Yorick at all.

He kept walking.

A burst, a streak of scarlet crossed his face—he jumped back, startled, fear coiling in him.

A cardinal perched on a branch nearby, looked down at him, cocking its head wisely to one side. "Purty, purty, purty," it informed him.

Angus's mouth twisted with the irony.

Abruptly, he frowned; he looked around him—and saw two long files of small new houses, only an occasional tree, no sidewalks, a lot of open land between houses, lots of room. The nearest one was dark, no curtains at the window.

Empty. A new tract house, waiting for a buyer.

Angus looked about, felt the sudden panic hit. He'd never been here before; he didn't even know where he was. And there was no one around, no one. Only an occasional car on the highway…

Car!

He leaped off the shoulder into the ditch, dropped to his hands and knees, cowering, trembling. He was alone; there was no one to protect him. There wasn't even a witness. They could kill him now and no one would know…

Then the steel of obstinacy clicked inside him. He lifted his head slowly, jaw tightened, glaring about him. Let them try! He'd stayed alive for thirty years before he'd met Yorick, and he would stay alive now. Let them try.

Blur of scarlet flashing down—the cardinal perched on a dry twig at the side of the ditch, head cocked, eyeing Angus with bright black eyes.

Angus's mouth twisted in a one-sided smile.

Saucy little devil…

Suddenly, his eyes widened and he lost his smile.

He rocked forward onto the balls of his feet, sprang upward in a frantic leap, up out of the ditch. He landed in a dive roll and kept on rolling until he could push himself up to his feet, running as best he could.

The sky tore behind him with a flash of ball lightning. Thunder blasted his ears, picked him up, threw him thirty yards, flung him aside in disgust. He heard it rolling away, booming and cursing.

Angus lay face down, clawing at the grass, trembling.

Then, slowly, he looked up, raising himself on his elbows, turned his head to look back over his shoulder…

A crater, at least twenty feet wide, tearing out blacktop, ditch, field…

Then the shakes hit, and the sick, rolling twist in the stomach.

A cardinal.

A fake. Beautifully done, of course. Beautiful. Remote-controlled carrier for a very small bomb.

It wouldn't have had to be very big.

Close.

Too damn close.

It flashed through his mind again: the cardinal's black bead of an eye, the frantic surge out of the ditch, the roll across the field.

He stiffened suddenly; something moved under the surface of his mind. The catapulting out of the ditch, from a stimulus that exploded… A sudden massive release of energy, catapulting mass, throwing it thirty feet… A straight line on the ground but a parabola in the air…

There was a twist to his vision, and the ditch was suddenly the timeline. The matter-transmitter was a rubber ball, bouncing back and forth from one side of the ditch to the other; but if you rotated the propelling surge at two right angles, the rubber ball shot up and came down well forward.

The words weren't right, the analogy wasn't really quite accurate, but he felt it, he knew it, he could wind it in wire; he had the concept now.

He could build a time machine.

Suddenly, he felt as though he were cocooned, trapped, locked into a future he hadn't really chosen, only let himself be pushed into. *No!* he screamed inside himself, and kicked his three-inch sole into the ground, set his teeth, clawed his fingers into the earth, and the angry negation boiled up in him: *Not yet! I won't build it yet! I won't!*

His anger wrenched a rift into the pathway to the future, opened a narrow channel leading straight to the empty tract house, and he knew it would stay open for as long as he wished it. He could walk straight down to that tract house if he wanted to, where everything was empty inside, and he could build it to his own shape and liking.

Angus smiled, beginning to relax, breathing more easily. He couldn't be caught. He would have to choose his future.

And he didn't. He kept his eyes on the tract house, the alternative, the life he wanted, the life he'd chosen on his own.

A sudden flash at one of the empty windows; a clot of earth shot into the air three feet to his right, pebbles stung his cheek, a shower of dirt; then the report, a loud, flat clap, harsh.

Angus knelt, staring, transfixed. A gunshot...

He threw himself flat and rolled as the second shot sounded, rolled and rolled frantically toward the crater, the only cover around, bullets tearing the ground around him. Pain seared his huge shoulder-muscle; he screamed, rolling, gunfire echoing, filling the world; pain ripped his arm, but he kept rolling, and there were more gunshots now, faster and faster, and...

He fell, howling in terror, for an hour, a second, eternity...

Earth struck up at his back, laid him flat, drove the breath from him; his head struck, hard, and the world swam about him.

Slowly, it settled and steadied. Silence rang in his ears; the only sound was his own hoarse, harsh breathing, out there, past the ringing in his ears...

The gunfire had stopped.

Then footsteps, quick, crunching in gravel, approaching... Angus tensed.

Yorick appeared over the edge of the crater, looking down, worried, grim, an old M-1 rifle in his hand.

Angus stared up, unbelieving.

"Y' okay, Ang?"

Slowly, Angus sat up. His right arm felt dead, his shoulder too. There would be pain there in a minute... He nodded.

"C'mon out, then." Yorick bent down, held out a hand. "They know there's no point in trying now."

Angus glanced at the rifle, swallowed, and grappled Yorick's hand and arm, pulled himself to his feet, out of the crater, Yorick half-lifting him. He stood shakily, one hand clamped onto Yorick's shoulder for support, and looked about him at the open field, the few trees, the tract house... There might've been ten snipers around...

But then, there might've been twenty GRIPE agents, too.

"C'mon." Yorick slung an arm around Angus's back, supporting him under the armpits, turned him toward the battered old Chevrolet.

Angus stumbled along with him, feeling guilty, ashamed, like a child caught being naughty. Just once, he wished, just once, Yorick would tell him he'd been a fool to go off alone, without a guard...

But the big man never would, of course. Angus's mouth twisted wryly. After all, that would be insubordination—wouldn't it? Even if Angus hadn't decided to invent the time machine yet, even if Angus hadn't decided to become Doc.

"It was worth it," he muttered, knowing Yorick would know what he was talking about. "It was all worth it. Because..."

The adrenaline ebbed just that little bit more, and the pain it had been blocking stabbed through—pain, sudden and scorching. He threw back his head, screaming.

Yorick frowned, turned...

And saw the hole in Angus's shoulder, and blood.

Angus had some very weird dreams while he was under the anesthesia. A myriad of faces, all his own, all lined and careworn but, other than that, identical to his, and all fifty years old: a business man, a farmer, a professor, an electrical engineer, a good husband and father living in a small tract house with a wife and a horde of kids...

At least he knew that one was impossible.

They swam past his face in endless succession but, again and again and again, one face out of all swam up to leer down at him, one face recurring, a face with a white lab coat below it, looking down at him with contempt and disgust. Each time Angus felt an answering anger and hatred, and the face would recede for a time, and the parade would begin anew.

A hundred, a thousand of them, some happy, some despairing, most barely content, or at least resigned: they were all the Anguses that could be, all the possible men that he could become—but only one of them would live, become real, the one that he decided would be.

The rest?

The rest would vanish as though they had never been—which, of course, they never would have. They were only potential, all of them, including the old bastard in the white lab coat.

That was the strangest dream, the most vivid, and it came back, again and again. Between that and the pain-killers they fed him all the next day, he could almost see the black haze around him, dark and palpable.

The day after, he came limping back home with Yorick's arm ready to grab in case he should stumble. He collapsed into the armchair in his bedroom and stayed there, the black haze still around him, unseen now, but there nonetheless. Angus simply sat, numb, drinking the mugs of soup that Yorick brought him now and then without tasting them, letting the shock wear off—but it was the dream that had shocked him more than the bullet.

Which one of those faces would he make real?

None of them! *Something inside him shouted.* I'm going to live the life I choose!

Which of course he would—and one of those future selves would thereby become real.

So he sat alone in the room while the afternoon faded and the twilight turned into night—there in the darkness, with only the light from a distant streetlamp, sitting, staring into space, hands lying useless in his lap.

Finally he rose, slowly, stiffly, and went out into the living room.

Yorick looked up from his newspaper with relief. "Feeling better, Angus?"

Angus didn't answer, only took down his coat from the peg and went out into the night.

Angus limped from one pool of lamplight to another, letting the black fog settle over his mind, letting random thoughts spin through, go wheeling away, reeling and laughing, howling derision at him. The parade of faces moved past him again, himself fifty years old in one suit of clothes after another, one hat after another.

Twenty yards behind him, there was a grunt, a sudden scuffle, but Angus didn't even hear it. He was aware only of the fragmented images in the darkness behind his eyes, the waves of chill shuddering through him.

He couldn't make sense of it. Any of it.

Behind him, a black-clothed man stepped out from behind a tree, lifting a strange-looking pistol.

Across the street, another man stepped into the light of a streetlamp, leveling a pistol at the first.

The first hesitated, but another man stepped out of the shadows on his side of the street, leveling a rifle.

Across the street, another man stepped out and lifted a rifle of his own.

The first man heard above him the sound of a rifle being cocked.

Across the street, a sizzle sounded, briefly lighting the face of a sniper in a tree; the muzzle of his weapon began to glow.

All the assassins looked at one another, shrugged, and stepped back into the shadows.

Angus walked on, unheeding.

Behind him came a parade of twenty sharpshooters, each with weapon ready, each watching for the slightest opening from the others, an opening which never came.

Finally Angus came to the lights of a business district. He stopped, mental images gradually fading enough for him to recognize a coffee shop. He went in; the door closed behind him.

The would-be assassins looked at one another, waited a few minutes, then quietly slipped back into the shadows.

Inside the coffee shop, the presence of other people, the susurrus of conversation around him, brought Angus out of his brown study and back into the world of the living. He looked around him, frowning, then down into his coffee cup—and suddenly realized his vulnerability. That's when he began to shake.

When the tremors had subsided, he stared down into the darkness of the coffee as though waiting for inspiration to rise. He sat in the corner with his token cup cooling before him, then remembered that light and company didn't necessarily make him safe and lifted his gaze, watching the few other people in the room very carefully, dread hollowing his belly, waiting for someone to take out a gun.

Somehow, he didn't want to go back outside.

He didn't notice that two of the other patrons were indeed watching him very closely—but were watching each other more closely still.

Fortunately, it was a coffee house that stayed open all night. Between the continual cups of coffee and the constant apprehension, Angus should have been on the verge of nervous collapse by sunrise—but adrenaline can keep pumping just so long, and Angus was still convalescent, so even though he had spent a long, sleepless night, he was strangely calm as the street outside lightened with false dawn. He finished his coffee, rose, and went out the door.

A minute later, the other two patrons rose too, as if by common consent, and followed him.

Angus turned his steps toward his apartment, then lost track of what he was doing, absorbed once again in the memory of that parade of fifty-year-old faces. If only he could find out which one would come to be, how he would choose...

He stopped stock-still outside an apartment house as insight struck. Of course! He could! He could find out how it all came out in, say, thirty years. All he had to do was build the time machine—and use it! He could destroy it after that one trip, if he wanted to.

Of course, he could do it *without* the time machine, for that matter—but on this issue, his sentry-host might be less than honest and, this time at least, Angus had to be sure.

So. It had to be the time machine. And he was the only man in the world who could build one, right now...

And he could. He was sure of that. He remembered the cardinal exploding, remembered himself shooting out of the ditch, and was certain.

For a moment, though, he was torn. Why should he take an advantage that was denied to the rest of humanity?

On the other hand, if he had to take all the disadvantages that went with being Angus McAran, why shouldn't he take the one big advantage with them?

Rage and resentment poured through him. Damn it, if the world was going to do all this to him, he was blasted well going to take it for everything he could!

He didn't even stop to wonder where Yorick was as he stomped through the living room and locked himself in his bedroom.

He got out the asbestos pad, the soldering iron, the tools, the wire. Then he sat down and started winding a coil.

Three hours, three new coils. Open the matter transmitter, solder in a few new resistors, replace the coils, link in a new rheostat and one hell of a big capacitor. He plugged it in, put away his tools, and sat down with his slide rule. A trajectory through the fourth dimension should require the same amount of power for the same "distance," after the initial surge that set it at right angles to the matter transmission trajectory... Angus frowned, slipped the stick, made some notes.

Half an hour later, he ran a few quick experiments, sending a sugar cube a minute ahead, waiting...

It didn't show up.

Angus scowled, turned down the rheostat, tried again... and again, and again, and again...

He got out the tools, hooked in a rheostat with reduction gear and, with the resultant fine-tuning, managed to get a sugar-cube to reappear after a ten-minute wait.

He hooked in a meter, took a reading, went back to the slide rule. Refigure, re-hypothesize, re-experiment—after four hours, he finally got results to match predictions.

He felt a cold chill on his spine. On house current only, he had a two-hundred-thousand-year-range. Apparently time travel didn't require quite as much power as he'd thought. Of course, that was only for the mass of a sugar cube, but still...

He scowled, thinking furiously... Of course! He was doing a flat trajectory now, not a bank shot off the chronocline... But could that make so very much difference?

His lips pressed tight. It didn't matter, did it? Theorize later; all that mattered now was that he had a machine that could take him where he wanted to go. He set the rheostat for thirty years, checked the terminals to make sure the polarity was future-ward (if he reversed the connections, he'd go back in time), and stepped to the center of the room, under the hanging coil, with the remote button in his hand.

Shouts, yells, from the living room. A series of muted, heavy thuds—silenced gunshots! A scream; running feet coming up to the door, stopping; the sound of splintering wood, more muted thuds…

Angus stared at the door, amazed it was still intact, paralyzed with horror.

He snapped out of the paralysis, limped to the doorway with the button still in his hand, threw the door wide…

Yorick knelt just outside, blocking the narrow hall, kneeling behind a barrier of a chair and a broken table (the top was chipped, and Angus caught the gleam of metal). Pencil-thin beams of ruby light speared over Yorick's head, through the wood of the chair, just missing him as he twisted aside, fired with a silenced automatic…

A shout of triumph down the hall; a ruby pencil charred wood near Angus's head, singeing his cheek. He jumped back, howling, and a ruby ray speared through the space where his head had been.

Yorick's head snapped up; he saw Angus and his face went livid with rage. "Go!" he bellowed, and his foot lashed out, cracking into Angus's hip-bone, slamming him back into the bedroom. "Get out of here! Get out, or we're *all* dead! Go on, get into the future, GO!"

"But…"

Yorick twisted aside just as a ray snapped through the wood. Another ray crackled over his head as a wiry, dark-clothed man dove over the barricade, gun hissing fire.

Yorick rolled, shot straight up into the man's chest. The enemy screamed as his dead body flew high into the air; as he fell, Yorick caught him, folded him up against the barricade. A sizzle, a stink of burned flesh…

"Don't you understand?" Yorick bellowed, somehow pleading. "Once you're out of here, they'll quit trying! Get gone! It's the only help you can give! Will you GO!"

Clap of gunfire from the living room, a scream in the hall… Angus slammed the door, leaped to the center of the room, pushed the button.

Metal walls, a foot to each side and a foot in front of him… Claustrophobia hit, then vanished as Angus turned and saw an angular, lined face above a white lab coat two feet in front of him, smiling sardonically. With a sense of horror, Angus recognized that face for his own.

"The time," the face said precisely, "is May 14, 4:23 P.M., 1986. Remember that."

Angus stared.

"My name is Doc. Dr. Angus McAran. And all you're going to find out from me is that you've just made your decision."

Angus stared, going rigid; then he screamed.

"Shut up and listen!" Doc snapped. "You've come into your own future to visit me. Not a possible me, not a probable me—the definite me, the *real* me. *You've chosen to make me real.* You've selected one of your many possible futures, your many possible future selves—me. Dr. Angus McAran. Doc Angus. You've made your choice. Now you get to live with it."

Angus had run the emotional gamut from shock to anger to cold hatred while Doc talked. Now his eyes narrowed to slits, and Angus's voice was level, emotionless. "It's not true. I can still kill you. All I have to do is destroy that first time machine."

"Oh, you can—but you won't, you know." The older man smiled sourly. "You won't believe me, though. So quit wasting my time." His hand moved outside the cubicle, as if to throw a switch.

Angus suddenly realized that he was standing inside a time machine—considerably more sophisticated than his pilot model. And Doc was sending him back. He jabbed at a button, and...

...Angus was standing, rigid with rage, in the center of his bedroom again. In the dark, with only the light of the streetlamp outside.

Angus frowned, looked around, puzzled. The trip hadn't taken that long, had it?

His gaze fastened on the coil that was positioned on the table. It was smaller than the one he'd wound that afternoon—and it didn't have the right convolutions...

A matter transmitter coil.

Angus swallowed, hard. The bastard had sent him back at least twenty-four hours, maybe more—before he'd built the time machine!

And he'd hadn't thought to build in a reverse circuit. He was stranded.

He could either re-build the time machine, or hide out until tomorrow, May 14.

But he couldn't hide out here. His twenty-four-hour-younger self was out roaming the streets right now—Lord! Only twenty-four hours ago?—but he'd be back tomorrow morning, to start building the time machine. And Angus didn't much like thought of *really* meeting himself.

He frowned at a new thought. How could he be sure it was May 13 right now? That old bastard Doc might have sent him back to May 12, or 11, in which case Yorick would be bringing Angus home from the hospital tomorrow, or the next day...

Angus stiffened. May 12. Two days ago.

Doc might have been lying. It was in his interest to make Angus believe he'd made his decision for once and for all. If Angus didn't decide to go through with inventing the time machine and finishing setting up GRIPE, Doc Angus would never have existed.

Well, Angus had made his decision, all right, but he could go back on it, Doc had admitted that—but did he want to?

He sighed, pulled on his coat, and turned toward the door. He wasn't going to think clearly in here, that was for sure.

Yorick looked up from his newspaper, nodded, and turned back to reading. Then his head snapped up, eyes wide. "How'd you get out of the hospit... Oh."

"Oh," Angus mocked. "What's the date?"

"May 12." Then, cautiously: "Uh... Ang?"

Angus stopped with his hand on the knob, looked back. "Yeah?"

"Need any help getting back?" Yorick seemed embarrassed. "I mean, we can have somebody who knows how to operate that first pilot model standing by."

Angus stood for a moment, thinking, then nodded. "Not a bad idea. Have him push the button at, uh..." He glanced at his watch; it was still clocking the time of May 14. "...6:15 PM."

"Will do." Yorick sounded very, very happy.

Angus glared at him, but the Neanderthal was studiously engrossed in his newspaper again. Angus snarled and turned toward the door again— then stopped, suddenly remembering. He turned back to Yorick. "Uh... there's a gun battle coming up in here tomorrow."

Yorick raised his head, frowning slightly. Then he managed to dredge up a weak smile. "Y'know, I'd almost forgotten about that."

"Uh... yuh." Angus studied Yorick's face a moment, decided not to ask how he'd come by the information. "Uh, you'll, uh... take precautions?"

"Oh, sure!" Yorick waved a hand airily. "Bullet-proof vest—and the coffee table's got a slab of armor plate inside the top. Won't stop a laser forever, but it slows it down quite a bit."

"Uh—yeah, sure." Angus felt a little light-headed. He turned toward the door again. "Well, uh—g'night..."

" 'Night," Yorick said cheerfully, returning to his newspaper.

Angus limped out the door, feeling numb. The promise of battle seemed to have been just what Yorick needed. Angus shivered. Some parts of this business, he was very glad he could leave in others' hands.

Maybe it was the promise that GRIPE, and Yorick, would keep existing. Angus held on to that.

He walked the darkened streets for an hour, so engrossed in analyzing the problem that he completely failed to notice the dozen scuffles he left in his wake. Finally he remembered Alasper and stopped, wondering how Yorick could cheerfully abandon this modern world and choose to live out his life in a Neolithic cave.

Then he remembered Nacha, and knew the answer.

It hadn't started out as something permanent, had it? Yorick had thought it was just one more assignment, and that Doc had his own reasons for wanting Yorick to make the hike across the Bering Straits Bridge, reasons that would strengthen GRIPE somehow, and the big guy had so much faith in Angus's future self that he had gone along with it cheerfully. Well, maybe not cheerfully, but at least willingly.

Then he had met Nacha, and known what those secret reasons were.

If Angus didn't finish setting up GRIPE, Yorick would die before his teens. He wouldn't ever be part of GRIPE, wouldn't ever meet Nacha.

Yorick was something completely new in Angus's life. Not just a time-traveler—a friend. Angus had never had a friend before. Not really.

But was Yorick his friend, or Doc's?

His. Angus had met Doc. He was sure the only reason Yorick liked him was because they'd been friends so long.

And a friend didn't abandon a friend to an early death.

Angus turned on his heel and headed back toward the apartment. Now he was so filled with zeal, with a fiery sense of purpose, that he never stopped to think what might be happening behind him—and of course he never looked back to see the silent spears of light that winked in the night.

Angus slammed into the apartment, ignoring Yorick's startled stare, and shucked his coat on the way to the bedroom-laboratory. He closed the door behind him, limped to the center of the darkened room, and stood waiting stiffly, trying to relax but failing, staring at the coil on the chair… waiting for the future…

An instant of dizziness, nausea, then…

Sunlight, gold and orange, the light of sunset—and the coil was larger, more convoluted. Angus squeezed his eyes shut, bowed his head. "What's the date?"

"May 14, 6:15 PM." Yorick's voice, gentle, somewhat tired.

Angus lifted his head slowly, turned to look at the Neanderthal, saw a stranger behind him at the improvised control board—and behind her, charred patches of wall, out in the hall. He swallowed with difficulty, remembering the battle. Involuntarily, his eyes went to the stain on the floor. He wrenched his gaze away, looked up to find Yorick watching him, trying to hide his tension and not succeeding.

Angus frowned. What was he waiting for?

Of course—a sign of commitment. So far, Angus could still change his mind.

But Yorick had gone through enough hell for him—Yorick, and all the agents he hadn't met. They had a right to a bond. He nodded, lifted his head slowly with a sardonic smile. "Who's the first time agent?"

Yorick let out a whoop of victory. Angus noticed that the woman at the controls had a radiant smile. Then Yorick leaped into the center of the room beside him, under the coil. "C'mon, Ang!" Then, to the woman at the controls, "You wired in the remote?"

"Right in here." She handed Angus a neat plywood box with a couple of knobs and a knife switch.

"Then set this monstrosity and let's go!"

"All right, all right," she said, grinning, and turned away to the control panel.

"When are we going to?" Angus asked.

"Tuesday, October 5th, 6:37 pm, in 82,684 B.C.!" Yorick crowed.

The woman set the dial. "Where?"

"Twelve miles south-by-southwest of Prague! Hurry!"

Angus watched her set other dials, one part of his mind identifying each one's purpose while another wondered at Yorick's impatience. Well, it was probably to be expected.

The woman at the controls stood back, waving.

Angus swallowed, lifted a hand in reply, and pressed the button.

They stood in the middle of a field with the golden light of late afternoon about them. Yorick looked around, his face strangely taut, then pointed toward a range of hills rising out of a pine forest, raw and eroded, with sparse clumps of grass. "There. Second hill from the left, on that ledge above the talus slope—about three miles away and a hundred feet up."

Angus glanced up at him, frowning, wondering at the tension in the Neanderthal's voice. Then he turned back to the remote box, set the dials, pressed the button.

They stood on the ridge; looking down the slope.

Yorick glanced at the sky. "Three hours ahead—toward the future."

Angus set the dial, frowning, hit the button.

The sun was down, but its glow still made the sky light. Dusk gathered beneath the pines.

"Nice evening for dying."

Angus glanced up at Yorick, puzzled by the irony in the big man's voice.

Then he stared.

Eyes still on the sky, Yorick was taking an automatic from a shoulder holster inside his shirt, an eighteen-inch barrel from his left trouser leg, a rifle stock from his right. He began fitting them together absently, eyes still on the sky.

Angus cleared his throat delicately. "You, uh… always carry that thing?"

"Huh?" Yorick glanced down, seemed almost surprised to find the completed rifle in his hands. "Oh… usually. Not always, though." He slipped a small telescopic sight out of his pocket, screwed it on.

Angus felt prickles at the base of his skull.

"There." Yorick nodded his head down the slope, hands still busy with the rifle. "That rock outcrop, near the stand of pine—see?"

Angus looked and frowned. "I see it."

Yorick nodded. "Nothing there now—but there will be. Watch."

After perhaps fifteen minutes, Yorick suddenly pulled Angus down behind a scraggly thorn bush, muttering, "There. Coming out of the trees at the bottom of the slope. See him?"

Angus looked, saw a stocky, wind-tanned boy limping painfully up the slope. He wore only a loincloth but carried a heavy spear. His forehead sloped, his brow ridges were heavy; he had no chin.

Neanderthal.

And he limped because his right foot was twisted to the side.

He looked terrified.

"His name is 'Aacthuu,' " Yorick said, low. "He's the joke of his clan; everyone despises him. His parents have told him, often, that they wish he hadn't been born—they've lost status for having birthed a deformed male. He's a burden to them and to the whole clan—but by tribal custom, he had to be given a fair chance to prove his worth, so his parents had to raise him.

"But not any more. This is the summer of his twelfth year—time for him to prove he's worthy to be counted among the men of the clan, by killing a saber-tooth with nothing but that spear. Worse, he's committed a heresy—he invented something."

Angus stared. He knew innovations had been very rare among the Neanderthals; they had kept the same technology for tens of thousands of years. To *invent* something… "What?"

"A bow and arrow," Yorick said sardonically.

A weapon of death—and a threat to everyone else in the tribe. No wonder the boy had been exiled.

But the intelligence that invention showed, the will that had pitted him against tradition!

"Nobody expects him to return," Yorick said. "In fact, they expect just the opposite—that they'll never see him again. And, frankly, they'll be happier that way." He spoke with a tight, sour smile. "He meets all the requirements, Angus. All."

Angus realized he was staring at Yorick. He shook himself and turned away to watch the boy. "You mean that if Aacthuu disappears, nobody's going to miss him. But there has to be more than that, doesn't there? He has to die without having affected the destiny of any other living thing. Otherwise, we change history, and who knows what effects that might cause?"

"Been thinking about it, have you?" For a moment, Yorick's smile was victorious again; then it curdled. "Any effects his life has had are part of the past already—and he definitely will die without affecting anything else. Just watch."

The boy had scrabbled his way up to the outcrop. As he tried to circle the boulder at its top, though, that twisted foot wrenched about, skidding on loose gravel and shooting out from under him. With a cry of alarm, the boy fell. He scrambled to his feet, but the foot collapsed under him again.

"He broke it!" Angus cried.

Yorick shook his head. "Only a sprain—but he can't get up again. Can't get up, so he'll have to fight from his knees."

"Fight who?" Angus asked in alarm.

The boy crouched behind the boulder, glancing warily over the top from time to time as he raked together the fallen leaves and sticks that had blown up against the granite. He took one of the sticks and began to rub it against the shaft of his spear, feverishly, almost in a panic.

Angus realized he was trying to light a fire—not just for warmth, but for a weapon. "Tell me! Who's he going to fight?"

"A saber-toothed tiger," Yorick answered, his face grim and set.

Aacthuu crouched behind the boulder shivering, fear knotting his belly. He knew the cat denned near here; he had found its spoor often. And this was the strongest place he could find near the den—rock for *some* protection, and open space for a clear throw. The wind was at his back; it must surely bring his scent to the long-tooth. He himself was the bait—and he couldn't stand, couldn't walk! He rubbed the sticks feverishly, as he had seen the shaman do, but no fire came! He shuddered, tried vainly to summon some anger.

The long-tooth prowled out from the trees.

Aacthuu saw it and tensed. Fear and the sureness of death lent him strength. If he must die, he would die a man.

Would anyone know? Or care?

Yes. Himself.

The long-tooth crouched.

Aacthuu set himself and, suddenly, the fear was gone.

The long-tooth sprang.

Aacthuu shot upright on his knees, arm snapping down and around. The spear flew straight and true, struck deep into the cat's breast. It yowled with pain—but the momentum of its leap carried it to Aacthuu. It struck hard, claws raking his chest, fangs slashing. He staggered back, tripped, and fell, curling his legs in. His good foot caught the long-tooth in the belly. He straightened his legs in one massive surge, hurling the cat clear of him, heard its body jar against the ground, snap. It screamed one last time before he felt the welling, sticky warmth at his throat, spreading over his chest, and saw the sky clot and fade.

On the ledge above, Angus pounded Yorick's shoulder, screaming, "Do something! You've got a rifle—use it!"

Yorick turned his head from side to side, his face granite, his body ironwood.

"Why not?" Angus screamed.

"For you."

Angus stared, horrified.

Yorick stretched out an arm, pointing. "There. Are you satisfied?"

His voice was so dead, so flat… Angus felt as though an electric field were playing about his back, his neck. He turned and looked.

On the slope below, the boy lay dead, his throat torn away, his blood a widening pool around him. Near him lay the saber-tooth, curled around the heavy spear, still struggling feebly.

"They're dead," Yorick said, his voice flat and harsh. "Both of them. Dead. Their life-lines stop here, knotted together." He turned slowly to face Angus. "Dead, out here, where no one witnessed but ourselves, where no one will find them but the vultures." He frowned into Angus's eyes, brooding. "So what if one of the bodies is gone? A few vultures will lose a few calories; so what?"

Angus turned away, looking down the slope.

"Will a few grams of lead make much difference to history, Ang?"

"No," Angus whispered.

"It's not too late to do something," Yorick said, voice low. "Not for us."

Angus bent his head and set the remote box for ten minutes in the past.

The long-tooth crouched.

Aacthuu set himself and, suddenly, the fear was gone.

The long-tooth tensed, gathering itself to spring…

Thunder shook the slope.

A ragged, bloody hole appeared where the long-tooth's face had been as its body shot backward, slammed to the earth.

Aacthuu knelt, staring, stupefied.

Then fear shot strength down his veins. He spun about wildly, seeking the demon that had struck down the cat.

They rose from a thorn bush on a ledge above him—not one, but two! One was surely a demon, bent, gnarled, flat-faced, jut-chinned, with earth-colored skins hung on its body—but the other was a man like himself, though it wore very colorful skins…

And they were coming down toward him.

Aacthuu cringed, knowing he was helpless before them. Would they now hurt him, after saving him? But if they would not hurt him, they would not be demons!

Aacthuu stared at them, struck by a new thought. Then he trembled anew. Were they demons, or… gods!

They came down the slope to the boy, Angus dazed and puzzled, Yorick's face wooden—but somehow, there was great compassion in the big man's whole stance and attitude. He knelt, slowly, a few feet from the boy, spoke in a strange, fluid language.

The boy stared, shocked.

Yorick spoke again, softly. Then he knelt, silent and waiting.

Slowly, the boy began to recover from his fear…

And Angus's eyes widened. He stared at the boy's face, then glanced at Yorick, then back to the boy. Chill and bony fingers stroked his spine, fondled the base of his skull. He couldn't be sure, he hadn't seen very many Neanderthals, so naturally they all still looked alike to him—but there was something about those two faces, something… He glanced back at Yorick, felt something akin to horror at finding that the Neanderthal was watching him.

Yorick's wooden mask finally broke in a sardonic smile. Slowly, he nodded.

Angus swallowed hard and looked away.

Yorick turned back to the boy.

Suddenly Aacthuu blurted. "You are gods!"

The Gnarled One looked puzzled, but the Man said, "No, Aacthuu. We are men, and only men. Like your father, like the men of your clan—like yourself."

Aacthuu hung his head in misery. "I am no man. I could not kill my long-tooth."

"You could have." The Man's voice was harsh. "But you'd have died in the killing of it."

"Then should I not have?" Aacthuu cried. "Should I have not died a man?"

The Man stood slowly, gaze still fixed on him. "You shall prove your manhood later, Aacthuu. We shall find you greater lions than this for your testing."

The Gnarled One spoke in a strange, ugly tongue.

"What's he saying?" Angus asked.

"He insists we're gods."

Angus snorted. "Then tell him he's coming to Valhalla."

The Man spoke again in Aacthuu's tongue. "You must come with us, Aacthuu. Our shamans will see your foot straightened. We will watch you grow to the fullness of manhood—and you shall prove that manhood in our service."

"The land of the gods!" Aacthuu breathed—then wondered at the way the Man's features twisted. But he gathered his nerve and cried, "I will serve you the whole of my life if you will take me there!"

"Why then, so you shall," the Man said quietly—and he bent down to gather Aacthuu up in his arms, almost tenderly.

Aacthuu clung to his neck, at first gingerly, then with a death-grip.

Yorick closed his eyes for a moment, letting the surge of emotion pass; then opened them to see Angus staring—but his face instantly went neutral. "Shall we go?"

"Not quite yet." Yorick's mouth tightened. "One small formality, Ang—this boy's no longer a member of his clan. He can't bear the name they gave him any more. He needs a new one."

Angus was suddenly wary. "So name him."

Yorick closed his eyes, shaking his head. "No, Ang. That's not the way it happened. The naming or him was yours."

"Damn it, it doesn't have to be that way!" Angus shouted. "That small a change won't make any difference!"

"It will to me!" Yorick snapped.

"Why can't *you* name him?"

Yorick felt Aacthuu cringing against his chest, remembered how terrified the boy had been when he heard the gods fighting, and lowered his voice. "Because if I had to name him, I'd call him 'Oedipus.' "

Angus's face froze, the muscles of his neck strained into whipcords.

He knew the name meant "twisted foot."

The two men stood glaring at each other.

Huddled against the broad chest of the Man, Aacthuu saw the two gods glaring at one another and trembled, for he knew who was hurt when gods fought—so he nearly fainted with relief when the Gnarled One turned on his heel and stalked away with a snarl that turned into words.

The Man stood in silence, watching him go, but Aacthuu could feel his satisfaction. When he looked down at the boy with a half-smile, Aacthuu plucked up his courage and asked, "What has he said?"

"The Gnarled One has welcomed you," the Man explained. "Your name is Aacthuu no longer. You shall be called 'Yorick' now, and shall be till you die."

"Eeoreeech," the boy repeated, wondering, for he knew what it meant to be given a new name. He was of the gods' tribe now! He was sure he would be only a servant, but he would be a servant in the household of the gods! "Eeyoreek?"

Yorick nodded, smiling. "You are Yorick now, and you will come with us to our homeland—and you will find that we are *not* gods, but only men, such as you yourself shall be one day." For a moment, he felt the full eeriness of the situation. "We have great knowledge, and you shall find that the Gnarled One is exceedingly wise, and we have things called 'machines,' such as the Gnarled One makes—machines that do marvelous things, such as taking us back to our dwelling."

The boy glanced at the Gnarled One, saw the gleaming square stone in his hand.

"That is the machine that brought us here, and which will take us back to our homeland," the Man said, his voice low. "It is a thing of magic… for we may not be gods, but we *are* magicians—magicians, even though we are only men."

Aacthuu shook his head, his gaze never leaving the Man's eyes. "You are gods," he said with absolute conviction.

Yorick sighed, reflecting that when Aacthuu had learned otherwise, he would remember that Yorick had told him the truth. His shoulders shook with a rueful inner laugh; then he said, "Believe it while you may."

He turned, carrying Aacthuu toward the Gnarled One, who was making strange motions at the machine. "How can we be gods," Yorick asked Aacthuu, "when we come from a machine?"

The Gnarled One pressed at the 'machine,' and the world went away—the old world, the world Aacthuu knew, but a strange, bright new world opened around him.

TIME AND TIDE

"A disconnection notice." Angus held up the red-lined bill as though it were Yorick's fault.

"We're not gonna manage to send time travelers very far without electricity," Yorick said. "But you can't blame the electric power company—we use a lot of watts just sending ourselves out of this cave."

They sat at a table in the time lab; its improvised walls hid the vast unlit cavern in which it sat. Some day, that huge bubble in the basalt of the Rockies would be filled with ten floors of bedrooms, offices, shops, a gymnasium, and a swimming pool—but so far, it only held a time machine, a table with refrigerator and hotplate, and white-painted plywood walls and ceiling to give the illusion that they weren't stranded in a huge space.

It was very secure, though. The only way in or out was by the matter transmitter built into the time machine.

"Safety costs," Yorick said. "Nobody can get at us here—but the power bill is incredible."

So was Yorick. He was a Neanderthal, adopted into GRIPE, Dr. Angus McAran's time-travel organization—then assigned to keep rival time agents from killing Angus before he invented the time machine.

Angus frowned. "The electricity will be a minor expense compared to buying this mountain and setting up our front organization—McAran Research, Inc." He couldn't help a glow of pride as he said it.

"Yeah, it is going to cost a lot, isn't it?" It was hard to argue with a genius, especially when he wasn't trying to win, just to make good sense. "Okay, so we have to start making a lot of money very quickly. How're we going to use this gadget to make a fortune or two?"

"Research," Angus explained. "There must be a hundred historians who'd love to have us find incontrovertible evidence of what really happened in their favorite historical eras."

"Don't tell me you're thinking of taking a film camera back to shoot the signing of the Magna Carta!"

"Nothing so crass," Angus said, "though it has occurred to me to sneak a very small audio recorder into the grove of Academe and find out what Socrates really told his students."

"Philosophers don't pay much," Yorick told him. "I was thinking of something more immediate—say, digging up buried treasure as soon as the pirate ship's out of sight."

"We'd foul up history, set up a time paradox." Angus frowned. "Unless it was a treasure that's never been found."

"There're plenty of 'em," Yorick said—then stopped, because Angus's eyes had gone glassy. "What're you thinking of now?"

"King John's treasure," Angus said. "I heard about it in 'Intro to European History'. Those last years, after Runnymede, he turned really paranoid, insisted on traveling all around the country to make sure his nobles stayed in line—but just to play it safe, he took the treasury with him."

Yorick stared. "The *whole* treasury?"

Angus nodded. "In a bunch of wagons. Of course, there wasn't all that much left, after he had to bail out Richard the Lion-Hearted and pay his ransom once or twice. At any rate, they were crossing a very shallow beach called the Wash—but nobody told him what happened to that beach when the tide came in."

Yorick grinned. "Let's go see, shall we?"

Fortunately, if they needed more agents, they could borrow them from the GRIPE of the future—and Angus made a brief mental-time trip to ask their twelfth-century Northern English agent to watch the approach of the royal train and tell Angus if King John changed his mind about trying to cross the Wash. He had to make the request ahead of time, of course, since the man had to hike a hundred miles to watch. Yorick had to make a trip out of the cavern to buy supplies, but it only took them a day to get ready. Then Angus waved good-bye, pushed the button, and watched the half-dozen wet-suited agents disappear. He took a coffee break, sat down to meditate, and waited for the twelfth-century agent to get in touch.

There was a commotion at the end of the street, and the travelers in the common room of the Golden Eagle looked up. One went to the door, then came back wide-eyed. "The king! 'Tis King John himself, surely!"

Most of the patrons leaped up and ran to the door, exclaiming.

Hugo stayed in his chair. "See the nasty little man who has drained England and made his reeves turn hundreds out into the snow? Why would I want to hustle to watch him?"

"Good or bad, he's a king!" the landlord took his apron off. "I've never see one, and I'm not about to let the chance slip by! Bestir yourself, lad."

Hugo grumbled, but he rose and went out with the others. He was a man on the young side of middle age, a yeoman on holiday, wearing a belted smock over cross-gartered leggings; there were a few white hairs in the mahogany of his beard, but not a one on his head. He had come to Thorp to buy sheep, for everyone knew their wool was the best in the North Country. No one knew he had really come because Angus McAran had asked him to.

There they came, a score of spears preceding the knights on their high horses, chain mail jingling, the sun gleaming off their helms, the gaudy paint on the shields slung at their saddle-bows making the king's progress festive. Behind them, in a litter slung between two more horses, came the king himself, waving with lackluster weariness at the people lining the streets. Hugo was shocked at how unimpressive he was—small, pudgy, ugly, with stringy hair and a sullen, glowering look of defeat. There was in him no trace of the golden Plantagenet handsomeness, nor of their delight in life.

Then the litter was past, King John was gone from sight, and one of the men-at-arms had dropped out of the procession to chat with a village lad who stood near the innkeeper as Hugo watched the wagons pass, drawn by oxen, moving slowly and deepening the ruts as they rolled. Their weight was clear, and the fact that each was covered with thick, strong cloth tied down along the sides should have made people wonder what was in them, if the rumor hadn't already run through the countryside that the king traveled with the royal treasury behind him. Hugo glanced at the villagers to either side and saw looks of greed and anger—greed for the gold, anger for the men-at-arms who marched beside each wagon and the knight who followed it with drawn sword.

The local youth finished telling the sergeant what he'd wanted to know; the man nodded in thanks, then pulled the lad in to walk with them. The youth looked surprised, but the sergeant's hand went into his belt-pouch and came out with a silver penny, which he pressed into the lad's hand. The youth grinned and marched happily in the train, proudly, even strutting a bit.

Out of the town they went, and the patrons of the inn turned to go back in. Hugo managed to catch the innkeeper and ask, "What did they want yon lad for?"

"To show them the way to the beach," the innkeeper told him. "They do mean to cross the Wash this day."

"I'll have a watch." Hugo turned back to the door. " 'Tis not every day ye have a look at royalty, and they do be going so slow I can catch them up easy."

"You'll have company enough," the innkeeper said with regret. "I'd come myself if I had not guests to feed."

"I'll tell ye if they do aught but walk." Hugo went back out.

Since the train could go no faster than the marching footmen who led it, Hugo had no difficulty catching up with the dozen locals who were following. After all, the train was the most exciting thing to happen in the village in the last decade, so they were determined to gain every ounce of entertainment they could.

As they went, Hugo listened to the villagers discuss King John's perfidies—high taxes and an overbearing manner, trying to tell his dukes and earls how they should manage their lands and treat their serfs. Not a one of them doubted for an instant that the severe hard times that gripped the country were the fault of King John, who had taxed every spare groat he could.

All well and true, Hugo thought; he'd had to start the high taxes to pay for Richard's ransoms, his Crusade, and his wars in France—but John had kept the taxes high even after Richard lay dead.

"Belike he paid the bowman who did shoot the Lionheart," one peasant said darkly.

"Aye," said his mate, "and be there any doubt he did have Prince Arthur slain?"

No, Hugo thought, but there didn't seem to be much evidence either.

"This country'd been far better off if good King Richard were here, it would," the first peasant said darkly.

True, Hugo noted, but the point was that King Richard was definitely not here, not in England, nor had he been for more than a few months of his reign. He'd been forever off to the next war or tournament. He was the very model of a knight errant, but he had never been much of a king.

A knight was riding beside the litter now, leaning down to talk to the king. Hugo wondered who he was and what they were talking about. Whatever it was, the king didn't want to hear it; he scowled, shaking his head, and swung his arm overhead and down, finger pointing ahead.

The stranger knight had been trying to keep him from crossing the Wash, Hugo realized, and frowned; this wasn't in the history Angus had told him. On the other hand, he had also said the historians never bothered with every last detail, only the important ones.

In the time lab of the 1960s, Yorick held up the top layer of a huge folded pile. "Okay, this is a seine."

"Looks like a net to me," Ella said.

There were four of them, all wearing wet suits, air tanks, masks, and fins.

"That's right, a net." Yorick nodded. "Only it's weighted along the bottom with floats on the top to hold it straight up,—so they call it a seine. It's also very big—and in our case, very, very long. This one has a finer mesh than most, to keep the tide from sweeping gold coins right through."

"So we're going to rig this thing from one side of the beach to the other?" Jobe asked.

"That's right." Yorick held up a mallet and a huge staple. "Drive these into the lower edge to hold it, then weight down the bottom even more with rocks, the biggest you can find. It'll catch the treasure. All we have to do is make sure that the net stays in place."

"And empty it after we've caught all the loot," Jobe said.

"Right." Yorick patted the circular bin that held the seine. "One load at a time. We fill this barrel and Doc will bring it back here. The headquarters crew will hoist it out and put in an empty, and we'll just keep the relays going until it's all back here. Any questions?"

One by one they shook their heads.

"Okay, turn on your air and let's go." Yorick put in his mouthpiece and turned his back. Ella started his air flowing, checked the meter. Yorick gave her the thumb's up sign as he pivoted back. The others turned on their air; each held up a thumb. Yorick turned to Angus with another raised thumb, and Angus hit the button.

In the thirteenth century, the surface of the Wash pushed up four huge domes of water that collapsed into waves, bubbles, and foam. The tide boiled briefly, then rolled on as it always had.

Below the surface, Yorick and his crew were busy, stringing the seine from one side of the beach to the other.

Peasants came from their hoeing to watch, lining the road to see their king pass by. No matter how they despised him, he was still entertainment. Following the royal train, Hugo heard one of the locals ask another, "Hadn't we ought ter tell 'un, though?"

"Nay," the other answered. "Let 'un find out for 'unself."

If it had been Richard, of course, they would have come forth in an instant—but then, with Richard, they would never have thought for a minute that they might have been punished for their impudence.

So King John's treasure train rolled ahead to its appointment with destiny.

Beneath the water, Ella finished hammering the last peg into the bottom of the Wash and swam over to Yorick, making the swab-O sign. Yorick nodded and handed her a bucket.

Hugo had gained on the royal train—in fact, he was close enough to hear the knight with the strange device on his shield say to John, "It is late, Majesty. Mayhap we should bide the night and cross at first light."

Hugo looked up in alarm. If they waited even fifteen minutes, they would see the tidal bore come rushing in like an express train.

"Rise at sunrise?" John shuddered. "And stay the night without an inn? Let my treasure stay out in the cold with only sentries to protect it? Are you out of your mind, Gorier?"

"Only concerned for your welfare, Your Majesty."

"But not for my gold's." John settled back against the cushions. "We must ford this beach this day."

"But the hour…"

"What do you mean, prattling on about the lateness of the hour?" John demanded. "The sun is still high in the sky! We march!"

"As Your Majesty will have it," Sir Gorier sighed.

Hugo relaxed. Perhaps this was the way events had originally happened, after all. Who would have written down a detail such as advice from an unknown knight?

Still, the knight was indeed unknown—and John was right, it wasn't even mid-afternoon. The treasure would certainly be safer for the night in an inn yard. Why would Sir Gorier be counseling him to wait?

"They have come to the ford, Majesty."

"Good." John nodded. "Proceed."

Of course, Hugo couldn't accompany them into the water—that would have been far too obvious; one of the knights might have cut him down where he stood. Worse, the sergeant might have pressed him into service, and Hugo had no desire to become a soldier.

The spearmen strode into the water without wincing, though their boots and leggings must have been soaked through in an instant—the water was knee-high. The knights rode after them, high and try astride their tall destriers. Then John's horses stepped in. The water churned a foot below the bottom of his palanquin, but the king was dry.

The first treasure wagon rolled into the water, then the second and third. John's horses were climbing out as the last wagon trundled into the ford. Across the Wash they went, the water lapping up to the hubs of their wheels. Hugo stared, seeing all twelve wagons in mid-stream, feeling the first touch of excitement as a distant rumble swelled into a roar.

There it came, a wall of water eight feet high, rushing toward the beach like an express train.

John turned to look, saw the tidal bore, and clutched his head, screaming—but the bellowing of the waves drowned him out as the water-wall slammed into the wagons. It bowled them over, surging onward, hiding the wagons from sight. Then it was gone, rushing away upstream and diminishing as it went. The water lowered and the wheel-rims were dimly visible above the angry waves. The tidal bore had overturned every single wagon.

Below the surface, Yorick and his crew were swimming about frantically. The seine was nylon; it held the weight as gold cups and plates filled it along with an avalanche of gold and silver coins—but some of the coins fell through and sailed on downstream, and as the net bulged, its lower edge pulled away from the bottom here and there, letting occasional cups and bowls squeeze through as the mounting weight behind them pressed harder and harder. Yorick swam here, swam there, snatching coins out of the stream. Then he saw a golden urn rolling along the bottom and kicked his fins to drive him over. He snatched up the urn, tucked it under an arm, and pushed coin after coin into it. Rings and necklaces sailed along on the current; he stuffed them into the urn along with the silver pennies.

Then, finally, the surge had passed. Yorick took the first of the stack of bins, handed it to Ella, and took one for himself as the rest of the crew swam over. Yorick put his urn into the bin as he dragged it over to the bulging seine and filled it with a cascade of gold and silver coins. With the bin in place, he swam back to the center of the beach, knowing the focus of the time machine would be on him as soon as he activated the call signal. Pressing against the middle of the net, he pressed the button—and the center of the net disappeared. Gold and gems hurtled down in an avalanche—but instead of dropping to the bottom, the cascade disappeared even as it fell.

The agents pulled the seine loose from the bottom as it emptied and swam back toward mid-Wash, funneling the treasure into the time machine's vortex. When the last of it was gone, they folded the seine around the few pieces left and swam into the vortex themselves. Yorick was the last to enter; the time-gate closed, and the tide rolled on as it always had.

John sat in the litter, his head in his hands, and Hugo could almost have felt sorry for him if he hadn't remembered the list of John's cruelties. The water was still so loud, though, that he certainly couldn't hear what Sir Gorier said as he rode up beside John's palanquin, pointing toward the waves. John only shook his head in despair, and Hugo breathed a sigh of relief; it would have been very embarrassing for local divers to have encountered frog-men. There would certainly be peasants enough diving for leftover silver pennies in the next few days, but if the chronicle was accurate, they would find very few.

In the time lab, Yorick landed belly-down on a heap of gold, feeling for a moment like a medieval dragon guarding a hoard. He pushed himself to his feet and went stepping and sliding down the ramp of treasure that spilled down out of the time machine to fill the lab. Walking across a beach of gold coins, he pulled out his mouthpiece and came up to Angus grinning. "Mission accomplished."

"I'll say it is!" Angus stared down at the piles of treasure in disbelief. "Uh—you don't suppose this is stealing, do you?"

"Stealing?" Yorick stared at him in amazement, then grinned. "No way, Ang! It's salvage, that's all. Check your history books—none of this was ever found."

"Yeah, and now we know why."

"Come off it." Yorick kept his grin. "You didn't see the way that tide was racing, Angus. It would have spread this loot all along that beach, and it was stirring up so much silt that most of it would have been buried that very day. The rest would have been silted over the day after that, and by the end of the week, it would have been buried deep. No wonder nobody ever found it."

"If you say so." Puzzled, Angus asked, "Why do you suppose a king would take his wagons across the shallows instead of building a proper bridge?"

"Too expensive," Yorick said immediately. "King John was a miser, Angus—didn't want to spend a penny more than he had to. Probably figured shallow water was all he could afford."

Angus still looked dubious, but said, "It's ours, then?"

"Hey, we worked for it." Yorick pulled a coin-filled golden vessel out of a bin and presented it to him. "A penny seined is a penny urned, Ang. Don't worry about the details."

"I suppose." Angus looked around him and finally grinned. "We have definitely increased GRIPE's liquid assets." Then he looked up with a frown. "You don't suppose this counts as money laundering, do you?"

"Well, Yorick said, "we really cleaned up—and according to history, it all came out in the Wash."

About the Author

Christopher Stasheff (1944 – 2018) spent his early childhood in Mount Vernon, New York, but spent the rest of his formative years in Ann Arbor, Michigan. He always had difficulty distinguishing fantasy from reality and has tried to compromise by teaching college. When teaching proved too real, he gave it up in favor of writing full time. He wrote novels because it was the only way he could be the director, the designer, and all the actors too. He tended to prescript his life, but couldn't understand why other people never get their lines right. This caused a fair amount of misunderstanding with his wife and four children. He seeks refuge in fantasy worlds of his own making, and hopes you enjoy them as much as he does.

Christopher died in 2018 from Parkinson's Disease. He will be remembered by his friends, family, fans, and students for his kind and gentle nature, willingness to guide and mentor any who asked, and for his witty sense of humor. His terrible puns, however, will be forgotten as soon as humanly possible.

MORE BOOKS BY CHRISTOPHER STASHEFF

WARLOCK OF GRAMARYE

Escape Velocity
The Warlock's Grandfather
The Warlock in Spite of Himself
King Kobold Revived
The Warlock Unlocked
The Warlock Enraged
The Warlock Wandering
The Warlock Is Missing
The Warlock Heretical
The Warlock's Companion
The Warlock Insane
The Warlock Rock
Warlock and Son
The Warlock's Last Ride

THE ROGUE WIZARD

A Wizard in Absentia
A Wizard in Mind
A Wizard in Bedlam
A Wizard in War
A Wizard in Peace
A Wizard in Chaos
A Wizard in Midgard
A Wizard and a Warlord
A Wizard in the Way
A Wizard in a Feud

THE WARLOCK'S HEIRS

A Wizard in Absentia
M'lady Witch
Quicksilver's Knight
The Spell-Bound Scholar
Here Be Monsters

A WIZARD IN RHYME

Her Majesty's Wizard
The Oathbound Wizard
The Witch Doctor
The Secular Wizard
My Son, the Wizard
The Haunted Wizard
The Crusading Wizard
The Feline Wizard

STARSHIP TROUPERS

A Company of Stars
We Open on Venus
A Slight Detour
The Unknown Guest

THE STAR STONE

The Shaman
The Sage

9 781953 215109